FLESH CRAVERS
A Forever Novel

Serendipity Bloom

DEDICATION

To my grandmother Maria. You would have loved this!

To my mom and dad who taught me to never give up on my dreams.

To the love of my life, who stood by me through this entire process; inspired me to continue, challenged me when I wanted to give up – patience of a saint!

To those of you (you know who you are) who listened to my silly ideas and still gave me the thumbs up, even if it wasn't your thing.

CONTENTS

ACKNOWLEDGMENTS

Thank you to my family and friends for supporting me through this adventure! I also want to thank all of my Kickstarter backers – because of you, I was able to make this dream come true. A special thanks to the following Kickstarter backers!

Wanda Soto
Iris
Cindy Pyle
Nikita Santiago

Crave:

To have an intense desire for.
To need urgently; require. To
beg earnestly for; implore.

PREFACE

Dear Diary attempt number one hundred and eighty seven,

Okay so here it is. My name is Sophia and I want to let you know one thing right off the bat - being dead IS SO NOT FUN! Now when I say dead, I don't mean all rotting corpse or ghost. I mean walking, living, breathing dead. How so, you ask? Quite simple - I am a zombie.

Very funny right? Do you have any idea how hard it is every day getting up in the morning to only see darkness? Wishing more than anything for just that one chance to experience the other side of the world? I do, and it stinks. This is my story as I live it. Maybe you want to join me on this adventure, maybe you don't. I will tell you how it all began and if you still want to come with me, I could sure use the company.

A little history lesson about zombies. It all stems from majick. Yes, you heard me - majick. Well, my breed of zombie anyway. There are many different types of zombies, but that's a story for another day. This is how my type came into existence. Apparently back before all was created or some crap like that, there was a witch named Hali who was the town hermit. Not even her sister took two glances at her without snickering.

Hali was a chubby little woman with a face like a bat and body like a sack of potatoes. Hali's sister Edna was the exact opposite. She was beautiful with fair skin, long brown hair with the natural hi-lights you would seriously kill for. She had a handsome fiancée named Jason

1

who would do absolutely anything for her. So needless to say, Hali had had enough and one night from within the walls of her cave, she decided to put a curse on her sister Edna. Why? Oh, this is the best part. Because she was jealous. Yep - just jealousy.

The curse was called "Forever". I know, it doesn't make sense to me either. Why would someone want to hurt their sibling because they were jealous? Well, Hali cursed Edna to live for eternity within the same body, never to age and never to die. Sound good? How about the catch? The catch is that while Edna would live forever she would be doomed to crave human flesh. No apples, no chocolate, no soda. Plain old human flesh. Of course, Edna wouldn't hear of having human flesh as food.

She tried everything to substitute - rats, rabbits, and even chickens. Nope, nada, zip. Edna cried and cried - she did not want to take someone's life. She didn't have the heart to tell Jason of the curse as she thought for sure he would not understand and leave her. Edna decided to see what would happen if she just stopped eating.

Besides, anything she ate made her terribly ill. What she did not know was that one of the repercussions of not living the curse to its full extent was disfiguration and rotting flesh. Your body just kind of falls apart on you - you lose a finger here and there, you lose your hair, maybe an eye and an ear. Kinda gross if you ask me.

When Edna lost her beautiful hair, Jason grew suspicious. He urged her to go to the town doctor, begged and pleaded, but Edna refused. She kept mumbling about her genetics and how she must have some sort of disease and nothing would

help her. As her body continued to rot, Edna
developed open wounds and oozing sores.

With Edna's denial to tend to her condition,
Jason grew distant. After a while, Jason could
not bear the sight of her and sure enough, he
left. Uh huh, you heard me right. He didn't only
leave her, but left town. Typical jerk man.

So, like any scorned woman, Edna decided she
would have her revenge on Hali. While Hali was
out and about in town, Edna snuck into Hali's
cave and managed to get ahold of her spell book
with full intentions on casting the same curse
on Hali. However, things didn't turn out the way
she had hoped.

Hali was a powerful witch and could also see
the future. She knew Edna would try a stunt like
that. She protected her spell book and when Edna
cast the Forever curse the tables turned back to
Edna. It made it so that every third generation
first born descendant of Edna's would
automatically be cursed with Forever upon their
eighteenth birthday. So NOT FAIR. And, what do
you know - Edna was pregnant. Big shocker.

Edna's daughter was named Eden. Pretty little
thing saw her mother fall apart and wither away
until all that was left was fleshy bones. Edna
was grotesque with bald patches of bloodied
clumpy hair on her head, sunken eyes and maggots
dropped from every thinkable orifice of her
body. Rot - what a lovely thing. Eden was only
a little girl of five when Edna finally had had
it and went to Hali and begged her to put an end
to it. Begged her to make it all go away.

Hali told Edna she could make it end but the
end was death. She would not get to see her baby
grow into a woman and marry. Edna was desperate
and told her she didn't care. She could not bear
to go every day wanting to eat her child. Craving

her flesh. It only took one night, you see, to make Edna go crazy - she bit Eden and took a chunk off her hand. Okay, not a chunk, a finger. Serious grossness right? Edna was so disgusted by what she had done but more disgusted that she enjoyed it. She wanted more. That's when she decided to let herself go.

She would absolutely NOT take the life of her child. After months of pure torture, Hali finally allowed Edna to come to her cave to end her life. So she did come up with a cure right? If you call death a cure, then yes. Hali brought Edna into her cave (of course she had to bring Eden too since her father didn't even know she existed). She put Eden to bed and carried what was left of Edna into her sacrificial room (I really don't remember what the room was called - didn't pay too much attention in history class. Boring).

The sacrificial room was huge, cathedral-like. Stone carvings of weird symbols only Hali knew the meaning of. Hali placed Edna on her altar and went around the room lighting candles. Once all candles were lit, the room looked very scary. Shadows danced around the room like entities in a haunted house. Creepy!

Hali stirred up a potion and whispered the words so that no one would hear. Edna wanted to learn so that she could tell Eden, but she just did not have the strength to do much of anything but lay there like a dead tree stump. Once all ingredients went into the cauldron, Hali stirred the concoction with what looked like a spinal cord.

Edna couldn't really see very well to be sure. One last whisper and one last pinch of some ingredient and voila! The room lit up like a torch and strong winds emerged from every direction. Hali's face was finally exposed and Edna didn't know what to say. Her sister was beautiful! She had flawless skin, high cheekbones, and beautiful long, black hair. Her eyes were solid black and her smile was ever so evil.

When Edna asked her how she had done it, she simply said "sometimes forever isn't all that bad." In that instant, Hali scooped up some of the potion in a vial and handed it to Edna.

"What are you waiting for?" said Hali. "Drink it".

Edna was confused. How had this happened? How could her sister be beautiful while she withered away?

"Will you promise to take care of Eden?" she asked Hali. "Please make sure you will protect her."

Hali smiled, perfect teeth gleamed beneath the candlelight. "Of course dear sister, I will take care of your precious child."

Just when Edna was about to drink the potion, she spotted out of the corner of her eye a small figure within the shadows of the room. She squinted to see Eden just standing there, wide-eyed and horror-stricken. At that moment she knew exactly what she must do. She leaped up onto Hali with any and all remaining strength she possessed and in one swift motion, opened the vial of potion and poured it down her throat.

Hali expressed a look of shock and then a loud wail emerged from her mouth. She clutched at her throat and gasped for air. She kicked and swung out at Edna but could not reach her. Edna watched her sister writhe in pain and as the winds of the cave became stronger, Hali's body began to disintegrate within itself. Edna leaped towards Eden and they made their way to the door.

As Edna shut the door behind them, they heard one final scream and then silence.

After a few minutes, Edna opened the door to see what had happened. Hali was nowhere to be found. The only thing that was left of her was a heap of her clothing in a puddle of black slimy goo. Once again, gross.

After this day, Edna and Eden lived in Hali's cave. Edna was determined to study Hali's spell book to find a cure for the Forever curse. While Edna was studying however, she had to consume human flesh. She found a spell in Hali's spell book that allowed her to travel by mirror. Almost like teleporting. Traveling by mirror has its benefits you know.

You can travel to far places to collect your flesh so that you would not clear out an entire neighborhood within a few years. Edna and Eden learned together by trial and error. Eden learned that her mother loved her and she was determined to help Edna collect her flesh to stay alive.

Anyhow, Eden grew up, met some guy, fell in love, blah blah blah and so on and so forth. You get the drift. I, of course, am her descendant. Here we are today, a gazillion years later and now what? How much have things changed you ask? Hah! That's a laugh. Check it out.

We live underground. Yes indeedie - like good ole great aunt Hali. Underground in a different sense though. Majickal underground. So anyway, I don't want to confuse you more than you already are. Let me make this simple - Spellbook + Study + Cave Art + Geeks + Lots of Years = Knowledge and Power. Our underground world is called The Lost Petals. Lame-o. Whoever came up with that name should number one be killed, and number two, be eaten - not necessarily in that order.

Anyway, The Lost Petals is a city for our kind. What is our kind called you ask? Ok. Ready for this? We are called Flesh Cravers. I know it sounds mean, but that's what we are. No sense in denying it. In our world, we don't just have Flesh Cravers though, but a whole array of species and humans as well. Yes, humans live with us too. Oh, we have the weird ones that enjoy pain and want nothing more than to satisfy the hungers of the Flesh Cravers. Don't ask now, that's a story for another day. Just remember what we call them - Pleasers. Sound like a nice name for them huh? Wait until you see one.

Okay, back to more important things. Humans, the real ones, do live with us in The Lost Petals. Family members who just can't bear to see their children go away. Lovers who want to make a life down here instead of up there. Up there? The human world, silly. You know that bright place where humans live? Where the sun shines every day and the stars shine at night? That wonderful place in which I wish to spend the rest of my undead life? Yep - that one. Bitter? You bet.

Now, I didn't really have a choice here. I didn't choose to be a Flesh Craver. It was my destiny. My curse. My punishment. Whatever. I don't really mind my life that much. I get to be eighteen forever. And on my eighteenth birthday, my mother gave me a family heirloom necklace with the Flesh Craver symbol on it. It's supposed to be a rite of passage or have special meaning. More stuff I really didn't care to learn about. The necklace was really pretty though. It's the powers I was more interested in.

I have some really cool powers. Hah! Intrigued right? Powers. Powers. Lemme see. I don't want to give it all away so fast. I can perform majick (whether I'm good at it or not is another story). I can sometimes change my appearance like change my hair or color of my eyes. I can read minds (super fun!). I can't read everyone's mind but if I try really hard, I can get at least some glimpses. And the last part of being a Flesh Craver – as long as we continue to eat flesh, we shall never age. We can be killed, but it's very hard to kill us. Let's just say go ahead and try. Most will fail.

Okay, this is my diary and I guess I should be honest. I stink at the majicks. I never really got the hang of remembering all of the spells. I confuse potions all the time, and to try to remember what ingredients go with what potion, come on! We should all be so lucky to be graced with a great memory. I, unfortunately, was not.

That's all I am going to reveal for now, but one last thing which I think is THE coolest thing. Traveling by mirror. Remember the mirror travel right? Well, that is how we explore and collect our flesh. It's called Reflectioning.

Oh, I forgot. I didn't tell you my job. Yes, we have jobs here. I am a Recruiter. In school, they made me take one of those stupid placement tests and they said, "Sophia, your test scores are impeccable for a recruiting position." And just like that, I was transferred from Withered High School after graduation (don't laugh!) to the tall building in the city called Financial and Legal Experts of Shrieking Haven (F.L.E.S.H).

I was stationed on the 68th floor with the Recruiting Division for Flesh Cravers. You thought this was just a curse, huh? Well, believe it or not, some people WANT to be Flesh Cravers. What do I do? I travel by mirror (Reflectioning). I am given assignments and

search for beings who want to join us down here.
How do they know about us? They dream about us.
They have visions of us. They sense that someone
will be coming for them. They feel out of place
in their own skin, in their own world. I offer
them a choice - come join us and journey to The
Lost Petals and become a Flesh Craver or walk
away and remember nothing. You see? Their
choice.

Most of the time, they choose to walk away
because they are scared. However, we do have
quite a few that jump at the opportunity for a
change in their life. So off to The Lost Petals
we go. I bring them through the mirror right
into the Recruiting Department where Orienters
are standing by waiting for their new recruits.

Now, enough about work. Let's talk about my
best friend Cecily. She lives in the next town
over called Fresh Waters. We have been BFF's
forever. Cecily is a River Fairy. River Fairies
look just like humans except for a couple of
things - they have kinda pointy ears and they
can breathe under water. Pretty nifty huh?
Cecily tries to teach me to swim all the time
but I am so afraid of drowning. Look - I KNOW I
can't die like that but that has been a childhood
fear of mine for as long as I can remember and
I haven't ALWAYS been a Flesh Craver, so there.
Let me have my phobia.

So anyway, Cecily and I spend all of our time
daydreaming (at night of course) about what we
would do if we could really explore other worlds
and dimensions the way we wanted to. I mean,
explore in the sense of not just doing it for my
job. If we were given the freedom to live like
a normal human again.

If we were able to go to college and date and
go out drinking and get drunk and go to parties.

I mean, we are stuck in our underworld world like prisoners. Before I became a Flesh Craver, I had a human life. And, I miss it. I miss it a lot.

Yes, we have certain freedoms and no we aren't being watched because, well, we just don't stray from this way of life. But seriously, I am getting kinda bored. We sometimes majickally text each other all night with silly little things like the latest gossip at school (yes, we have to continue to take classes on the principles of F.L.E.S.H. and move into the next levels of majicks), or talk about the newest recruit fruit loop I found. We go to the movies and pretty much live life like humans, so don't judge us too quickly.

Cecily still lives with her parents since they age very slowly. Basically every River Fairy year is like 100 human years. They do die though and there are several ways to kill them. This was one of the parts in history class I actually paid attention to since Cecily is my best friend and I really didn't want to do anything that would kill her.

River Fairies are super sensitive. For example, sunlight is a big no-no. Instant death. Poof. Gone. Disappear forever. Also, give a River Fairy a peach and they swell up like a balloon. Severe allergies to peaches. Go figure. There are other ways they can die, but I don't want to get into that right now.

Love life you ask? Hah! That's so funny. I have had approximately one boyfriend since my arrival to The Lost Petals, and he broke my heart and I wish I had never known him. When did he break up with me you ask? Forty years, four months and 8 days ago, but who is keeping count? His name is Max and wow, I hate him.

Well, I don't really hate him but he crushed me so badly. He is an Angel. Correction - a Serminian Angel. We dated for seventy years, happy, content, did I mention HAPPY? When all of a sudden he got this message from this heavenly father who shall remain nameless that he had to go on some sort of mission to save some souls and whatnot. He left for the greater good. We had a good life together. No children, well, because Angels can't have children. I was totally okay with that because I was so not ready for a baby. I mean I AM only eighteen right? Ignore the part of me being over 110 years old. That is completely irrelevant at this point in time.

Off on a tangent I know. He just left me. Said he hoped we could be together in another realm. What the hell was THAT supposed to mean? He never explained it to me and did not give me the opportunity to ask. He closed his eyes and was immediately transported by his guiding light. Whatever. Moving on.

I will try to update this diary as much as possible but as you can tell, I have a pretty demanding job. Recruiting is not all fun and games. It takes serious skill and training to get to where I am and I guess I must sleep sometime right? Good night dear diary, until next time.

1 SURVIVAL

"Well, what do you think? Should I wear the striped pants or the solid pants? C'mon Cecily, just be honest."

Cecily just stood there looking at me as if I had two heads.

"I like the striped ones better" she said. "They make you look thinner."

Great. Just great. Cecily had the perfect body - petite little Fairy. Me? Greedy Flesh Craver. I have been steady in a size 12 for a very long time. I am five-foot-five, have medium dark brown hair a little past my shoulders. My complexion is pale, paler, and palest. My eyes are brown and I wear glasses. Sure, I could just use majick to get rid of the glasses, but I have to have SOMETHING to distract from my other not so great features. Look at me go.

"Cec, I want to look professional for my new recruit I don't want to date him," I snapped.

My boss Evan called me earlier today to give me a lead on a possible recruit. Twenty-two year old male with ESP. Very quiet, and a loner. No friends because everyone thinks he is a freak. The perfect candidate. No one will miss him. No one will care. "Really Sophia I just don't understand why you aren't out there playing the field. I mean it has been over forty years! GET OVER HIM!" Okay, so Cecily does not have a way with words, but she does have a point which I will NEVER admit. "I know Cec, but I just don't want to get hurt again. I know Max is out there somewhere, probably with a pretty little Angel wife with pretty little perfect Angel wings and a pretty little perfect Angel smile. And he's probably very happy and not thinking about me. But I can't help that all I had ever known has left this big giant gaping hole in my heart. Sorry, I just need a little more time."

I posed in the mirror with the striped pants and decided to go with the solids just for sheer principle.

"Do you think he's cute?" I asked.

Cecily threw her hands up in the air and simply said, "I give up." I loved doing that to her.

On my way to the office, I picked up a newspaper and read the headline.

OLD LADY MAMIE SPOTS UFO OVER MEADOW FIELD

Ok so number one: Old Lady Mamie is like a bazillion years old. Number two: she had let herself go for so long without flesh that she lost one of her eyeballs to rot and the other eyeball is half gone. Number three: For Old Lady Mamie to see a UFO in our world would be like, I don't know, me finding a needle in a mound of flesh. What some people will do for free flesh.

Apparently, if you give a good enough story to the paper and it actually makes front page headlines, depending on who you are, you can get some pretty sweet free stuff. For Flesh Cravers the prize is free flesh. This is where the Pleasers come into play. I still say gross.

I walked up the steps to F.L.E.S.H. and ran into Sam because big surprise, I wasn't paying attention to where I was going. Sam – twenty-four, and totally in love with me. I don't want to sound unappreciative or anything, but Sam is just not my type.

First, he is about two inches shorter than I am and when you look closely at his hair, you can see mounds of dandruff. And too, his breath smells bad. I think he doesn't feel the need for personal hygiene just because he is a Flesh Craver. I know the value of good breath. He apparently does not. He was one of my recruits several years ago and from day one wanted nothing more than to establish a relationship with me.

"Hi Sophia," he said with a cheesy grin on his face.

Under the lights of the lanterns outside of the building, his face kind of glowed. Not the nice sweet glow, but the type of glow that creeped you out. That yellowish tinted glow that looked like the tail end of a bruise.

"Hi Sam, how are you doing today?" I asked, not really interested but trying to be polite nonetheless.

"I'm good, good thanks for asking. Hey Sophia, I was wondering if you would like to go with me to the movies on Friday night. There's the new horror film Attack of the Dog Face Flesh Craver or the romantic comedy Until We Meet Again. What d'ya say?"

What I WANTED to say was HELL NO and keep walking but in an effort to not hurt his feelings as usual, I did what any normal person would do – I lied.

"Sam, I can't on Friday night. I have a thing with Cecily and her family and I absolutely can't miss it or she would have a fit. Maybe some other time?"

And there I said it. The ultimate trap. Maybe some other time. The invitation for him to ask me, yet again, to go out on a date with him; the opportunity for me, yet again, to think up a lie and turn him down.

"Uh, ok, sure, maybe some other time" he mumbled.

I saw the look of disappointment on his face, but I couldn't help it. We said our goodbyes and I stepped into the elevator. I can't spend the rest of the day feeling sorry for him. We go through this at least once a week. Off to work I go.

It's funny because you think the 68th floor and you think a very long ride. But, in our world, things move a lot faster. Majickally faster. Our elevator is like another teleporting device that works telekinetically. Think what department you need to go to and there you are. Step in and step out. Doesn't give you much time to do much mingling but helps when you are running late.

Evan spotted me as soon as I stepped foot off the elevator and that told me one of two things - either I was in trouble for not completing an assignment or he had a favor to ask of me. Peachy. I avoided eye contact as long as possible and maneuvered my way towards my cubicle.

"Sophia I'm so glad to see you," said Evan.

"I wanted to speak with you before you went on your new recruiting case. First, let me tell you that I think you are doing a fantastic job and I am certainly keeping my eye on you when we have an opening for the next Recruitment Senior."

Oh no, here it comes. The inevitable favor was about to come spewing from his mouth.

"I just have one favor to ask of you. Can you please take a newly turned out on their first collection? Her name is Chloe and she is scared to death. She has only traveled once on her own and she ended up making a mess of things on the other side. She scared the bejeezus out of the potential victim. She woke him up out of a sound sleep before she was able to recite the sleep continuing spell."

"He was an old man, survivor of one of these silly wars these humans have and had a nice gun under his pillow. He shot her on the side of her head nearly taking her head off. She fell up against the mirror and shattered it and she had to run through the entire house looking for another mirror so that she could get back home. She ended up traveling from a bathroom mirror that was more rust than mirror. Davis had to go back to the potential victims' home and finish the job for her."

"She is very self-conscious about her appearance because part of her head is missing and you know she won't heal until she eats. Henderson called out sick, said he had a craving for a hot dog and now he can't seem to leave his bathroom. What do ya say?"

Sigh. What COULD I say but yes?

I mean, I remember how petrified I was the first time I went on a collection. To remember to recite the spell perfectly and to not wake the potential victim. To choose the perfect body part. So much pressure.

"Where is she Evan? This had better not take up my entire day. New recruit lead remember?"

"Thank you so much Sophia," he said.

"I knew I could count on you. She is just sitting over there waiting for you. I told her you would be the one to take her since she seemed to want a woman to take her this time. Thanks again and keep up the good work."

End of conversation. Goodbye Evan, just like that.

I walked over to Chloe, and boy, did she look pathetic. No wonder she was self-conscious. She was a freakin mess. Her hair was disheveled, and yes indeed, part of her head was missing.

"Hi I'm Sophia and I will be your collection coach for today. Henderson is not feeling too well so ya got me."

Chloe looked like she had seen a ghost.

"Um, hi. I'm Chloe. I don't know if I can do this. I think I am going to be sick."

Before I could blink, she opened her mouth and threw up all over me. It wouldn't have been so bad except when we throw up it is very different than humans. We throw up blood. Coagulated, smelly and sometimes black blood. Not a pretty sight. This excretion is well known as glomulis.

"I'm so sorry," said Chloe.

I didn't want to be mean to her but now I had to change.

"It's okay Chloe. We have all been in your position and I completely understand." She gave me a half-hearted smile and looked down. This was going to be a long day.

"We will just go to my place so that I can change and we will be on our way to your collection site."

We could have taken the elevator back down and walked to my apartment, but I seriously did not want to walk around drenched in blood. Chloe followed me over to my cubicle and sat down. I walked over to my 1930's style Victorian mirror and uncovered it. Chloe's eyes almost fell out of their sockets when she saw it.

"Um, are we going to travel by mirror right now?" she asked. "Chloe listen - we have to go to my apartment so that I can change my clothes and frankly you should change yours too. We don't have much time until potential victims start waking up to go to work so we really need to get a move on. You are going to have to start getting used to traveling by mirror. It's not that bad. Let me show you."

She looked like she did not believe me, but she took my hand and stood next to me.

"All you have to do is take a deep breath and recite the spell," I said.

"Repeat after me: Myfirio Teithio." As soon as Chloe repeated the words, we were instantly taken down a spiral path through the mirror.

It is funny sometimes the way we travel. With mirror traveling (called Reflectioning, remember?), you are kind of taken through a journey into your mind. You see images all around you, floating with you as you reach your destination.

I often see myself in the human world with a family – husband (although I could never really see what he looks like), children, white picket fence and a dog. I also see Max (and he is usually standing there with his perfect Angel wife). At times, I see very disturbing images like the gnomes of the Mayron Dimension. Yes another story for another time.

So, I held Chloe's hand and we traveled together. She kept looking over at me as if she was not sure of what to do next. Oh, the newbies are so funny. All in all the travel takes approximately three seconds however can feel like a lifetime depending on how you want to handle your visions.

I don't like to linger too long - it's very easy to get lost in Reflection World. I have heard some stories of people that never made it back. I don't know, maybe it is nice to just stay there and live a happy non-existence? Sounds scary to me.

When traveling with other people it can get a little tricky because you are seeing their images as well. This one time I traveled with Henderson and I got a glimpse of his mind - he was a young boy of maybe eleven or twelve and was playing with a rogendard (this is a tool used by Wentinian Angels to remove ligaments from the body) on a dog.

He was smiling as he was doing this. When we had returned from our trip I asked him what it was we had seen and he simply stated, "Reflection World images are not all real." He left it at that and so did I. I try to stay as far away from Henderson as possible. He just gives me the creeps.

The trip with Chloe was nice. Her images were of dancing Lady Mallies (the female only species of fairies that live inside teardrops). They were beautiful - brilliant colors of orange, pink and purple flowed around us like ribbons of satin. As they circled us, their wings fluttered so quickly they were almost translucent.

I could smell the cool breeze their wings created, the scent of fresh lavender. I smiled at Chloe as we exited Reflection World and entered my apartment.

A quick cleaning and change of clothes for both of us (although I did not know what to do about the nasty oozing stuff that was sludging down her body from the missing parts of her head), and we were off.

I ended up giving her a scarf to put over her head to hide the gaping hole and control some of the mess. We stepped in front of my hallway mirror and Reflectioned to the home of her potential.

We passed by some more Lady Mallies and of course, there was Max holding his perfect Angel wife's hand. Anyway, why was she so pretty? Tall, long dark hair. Thin. Petite. Her wings had a gross tinted hue of pink when they glowed. Okay, not gross, but I wanted her to look gross. She looked, I don't know, heavenly. Whatever. I'm over him. I'm over him.

We exited Reflection World and entered the home of Chloe's potential victim. Now, the fun begins.

2 CHLOE

Once we exited Reflection World through the mirror and entered the potentials' bedroom, I felt an immediate rush of excitement. It is hard to explain the deep hunger for human flesh.

"Chloe, the potential is asleep now. We want to keep it that way," I whispered. "In order to do that, we must recite the sleep continuing spell. Can you remember what that is?"

Chloe looked at me seemingly lost and I swear, on everything unholy, she was going to throw up again.

I helped her out a little. "Okay, repeat after me – Somnus Altus."

She repeated the spell and the potential glowed for a brief second and that was all we needed to see to know that he was meant for her, and that he would not awaken.

Chloe glanced my way and whispered, "Is he going to wake up?"

"Once you say the spell, the potential will not wake up or feel any pain. That is the point of the spell. Now Chloe, listen to your hunger and tell me what you are craving."

Once again, a blank look emerged from her face.

"What do you mean listen to my hunger? I am

starving! Can't I just take a bite or something?"

Oh boy, this was going to be a lot harder than I expected. Damn Henderson for not teaching her the basics of collecting!

"Okay, I see we are going to have to start from the beginning. Did Henderson go over with you the Essentials and Fundamentals of Flesh Collection?" I asked.

"What's that?" she asked with a confused look on her face.

Wait! Hold on for just one minute! Did she just ask me 'What is that'? Oh my freaking Goddess!

"Chloe, THAT is only one of the most important user manuals you will ever need being a Flesh Craver. THAT is your guide to surviving on the planes. THAT is YOUR BIBLE!"

I practically shouted these at her and I know I should not have taken it out on her, but honestly, this was ridiculous.

Here we were at a potentials' home, ready to collect, and she had no idea what she was doing. No wonder she got half of her head shot the hell off last time! Angry and frustrated, I took Chloe by the hand and started dragging her back to the mirror.

"Chloe, I don't think we should be here now. There is a lot for you to learn about collection and you are not ready. We need to go right away."

I quickly said "Nevrii" and pulled Chloe in towards the mirror. "Myfirio Teithio" and we zipped back to my cubicle. Now I was pissed.

Back at the office, I introduced Chloe to Summer, a resident human who donated flesh to newly turned Flesh Cravers. Summer took Chloe by the hand and they disappeared into the elevator. From there they will go up to the seventy-sixth floor - the feeding wing.

All kinds of feedings take place here and one of the sections is specifically for Flesh Cravers. Chloe will be just fine. Once she eats and is all healed up, she will be back with Henderson and he can continue NOT showing her the ropes. That lazy bastard!

I walked over to Evan's office and he looked up from his desk.

"Back so soon?" he asked. I smiled. I couldn't help it.

"Shit Evan, Henderson didn't even have Chloe study Essentials and Fundamentals of Flesh Collection! How in the world could he have sent her on a collection by herself?" I asked.

"Sophia, I can't believe that Henderson would have sent Chloe out on her own without having reviewed that with her. Let's wait until he gets back in the office to ask him firsthand. She could be lying because she was scared."

Sigh. He was always giving Henderson the benefit of the doubt.

"Whatever Evan, I am going to go get ready for my new recruit lead. Remember that?"

He just shrugged his shoulders, looked back down at some paperwork on his desk and continued what he was doing. Typical.

I went to my cubicle and checked my messages. One new voicemail. Do I have time to listen to this message? Will I have to help someone, making me even more delayed for my new recruit lead? Not wanting to take the chance of missing this lead, I ignored the message. Whoever it was, they obviously did not have an emergency or they would have called back or tried to reach me some other way. Off to my apartment.

I decided to walk this time. Didn't really want to see Max with his stupid gorgeous Angel wife, living happily ever freakin' after.

Walking the streets of The Lost Petals can get spooky if you do not know where you are going. For example, one block away from F.L.E.S.H. is an alley inhabited by Pleasers.

Not just an alley though, more like a small community. The Pleasers sometimes creep out of the shadows covered in their cloaks to mask their hideousness and beg a Flesh Craver to take them. You hear things like "please, I will do anything, anything if you would just take my flesh" or "you have never had flesh as tender as mine." Some of them make hissing sounds like snakes when Flesh Cravers come around as if they smell something wonderful. So extremely creepy.

The Pleasers are not nice humans. Most of them are disfigured because of all of the flesh they have lost, and many of them have more than one part missing. Remember, they don't grow their parts back or heal like we do.

Some have connections to sorcerers who will heal their wounds, but they must pay a price. Sell their souls; give up their first-born children, etc. They are grotesque and unbelievably dangerous. I have warned many a new recruit to stay away from Pleasers Run unless they wanted to be mauled and forced to feed. Some of them listen, some of them don't. Up to them.

There were several occasions where Pleasers kidnapped a Flesh Craver and tortured them by forcing feedings on them. We can't die easily but we do still feel pain and do still get sick. Me personally? I was heading in the opposite direction. Didn't even want to risk running into one of them.

My apartment is small and on the second floor. It is a one-bedroom apartment with a living room, dining room, kitchen, and bathroom. I have a balcony with fresh herbs in pots (not as if they get any sunlight, we have to use artificial light here), and a small potted apple tree. I don't eat the apples, but sometimes take them with me when I go after my recruit leads. You never know, they might be hungry on the way.

As I stepped up to my apartment door, I heard a strange sound coming from inside my apartment. Instantly, my mind raced to the many spells I have learned throughout the years to protect myself as I unlocked the door.

I whispered "caecus" and felt my body disappear almost immediately. I loved this invisibility spell! Okay, it does not actually make me invisible, but it "blinds" other beings from seeing me.

I walked into my apartment and looked around; quietly creeping from room to room looking for the source of the strange sounds I had heard. Entering my bedroom, I spotted a very short figure rummaging through my closet.

I let out a small sigh of relief and whispered "san caecus." This would make me visible again.

"Sormy, what are you doing in my apartment and why are you digging through my stuff?" I asked.

"Hi Sophia, I-I-It's nice t-to s-s-s-ee you again. I was j-j-just looking for a fresh t-shirt."

All right, so Sormy is a closet troll. Closet trolls live in, well, closets. They travel through portals opened by a small rock they carry on a necklace. The rock is made of zaphin, a very rare metal the closet trolls claimed a long time ago on their plane of existence.

No one else has access to zaphin. Many have tried to follow the trolls when they open the portal in an attempt to steal even the smallest grain of zaphin only to find a horrible death awaited them on the other side.

I really didn't think the rock was all that important and always made sure I let Sormy know I had no intention of following him to find out where they stored them.

"Sormy, I have told you a million times. You can't just barge into my apartment and take my clothes. If you need or want something, all you have to do is ask and I will be more than happy to give it to you."

Sormy glanced up at me with his beady little eyes and giant crooked nose. "T-t-thank you Sophia. I'm s-s-orry to be so much trouble." Once he said that, he put his head down, brought the zaphin to his mouth and whispered his incantation to open the portal and poof, he was gone.

Sormy is one of the nice ones. He found me at F.L.E.S.H. one day and helped me pick up a pile of paperwork that had flown out of my hands during one of my clumsier mornings. He was testifying in a court case at the time and was extremely nervous.

I helped calm his nerves. Closet trolls usually take small articles of clothing, something so insignificant that most people wouldn't even notice they are missing, or justify in their heads some silly story of how their other sock went missing.

With Sormy gone, I went to the bathroom and turned the shower on. I still had some of Chloe's goop all over me, and boy did I smell bad! I hopped into the shower and immediately felt relief and relaxation. I was so exhausted! I hope that my recruit lead will not be a waste of my time, kind of like Chloe was.

Into a pair of blue jeans and a white knit sweater with blue stripes and I was off to meet Jeremy Hindle. I guess I had better study his case file before I go.

3 JEREMY

Case file of Jeremy Allen Hindle

Full Name: Jeremy Allen Hindle
Address: 843 Golden Gates Road Scranton PA
Phone Number: 570-444-7835
DOB: 3/17/1985
Height: 5'8 Weight: 170lbs
Occupation: IT Service Support at Xerint Technologies; 3 Years
Medical History: Chronic Migraines, Fractured Wrist at age 14
Medications: Tylenol
Family History: Both parents deceased; car accident in 2001. No siblings. No other family members located
Mental Health: At the age of 15, Jeremy attempted suicide by wrist slitting. Attempt unsuccessful as he did this at school and he was found by other students. He was hospitalized and rehabilitated. There have been no other reports of attempted suicide since.
Lead Information: Jeremy has been monitored for 2 months due to strong psychic energies released when his migraines occur. It has been determined Jeremy is a precognitive experiencing visions both in dreams and in waking state. His visions are usually followed by massive migraines. Daily monitoring has identified Jeremy has been having visions at

least two times per day. He keeps a written account of each vision in a small notebook and completes investigations to try to prove his visions wrong. He is a quiet, sometimes shy individual, with no known friends or acquaintances. Previous romantic relationships lasted no longer than a couple of weeks with the female leaving for "it's not you, it's me" reasons. In Jeremy's documentation within one therapy session, he stated he is convinced he cannot hold a romantic relationship because of his visions.

Daily Itinerary: Jeremy holds a routine schedule. Wake up at 6am, shower, cup of coffee, off to work. Work 8-5 with one hour for lunch. Usually goes to the local deli and orders a BLT on Rye and a coke. Travels by car. Goes shopping once a week. Parks his car in his garage. Owns his home, which was willed to him to receive on his eighteenth birthday. Has some cash in the bank - net worth approximately $25,000.

Pets: Has one cat named Munchkin. Siamese, 2 years of age.

As I browsed through the case file, I noticed an array of snapshots of Jeremy. Average looking guy. In each photo, however, I could not get a good look at his face. His hair seemed to always hang over his face, blocking it from view. Okay well I guess I should get going. Wouldn't want to be late now would I?

"Myfirio Teithio" – off through Reflection World. Hi Max and beautiful Angel wife who I do not know and probably doesn't exist but I can't stand anyway. Ugh. Why do I always see him? Get over it Soph. Destination reached.

I entered the dark room from his closet mirror. Something hissed at me almost immediately.

"Hi Closet Troll. I promise I am not here to take anything from your territory. I just need to get into the other room." The troll looked at me as if to study my face, grunted in disgust, kissed his zaphin and he was gone. They are so touchy!

I opened the closet door into another dark room. Doesn't this guy own light bulbs? As I entered the room, I ran into something hard and soft at the same time.

"Ouch" I whispered. That was my knee.

"I knew you were coming tonight."

Oh my freaking Goddess! Since I was so distracted by my injured knee, this voice from directly in front of me scared me so badly that once he turned the light on, I realized I had walked right into him.

The light threw me off balance and I tumbled onto the couch. Idiot!

"Hey, are you okay?" he asked.

I quickly steadied myself and got back to my feet.

"Sorry, yes I'm ok, thanks. That was not very nice of you to sneak up on me like that," but really, who was doing the sneaking? I mean I did just enter HIS home from his closet right?

"Sorry. I just thought you could only enter in the dark is all," he said.

"Allow me to introduce myself. Jeremy Allen Hindle. Please just call me Jeremy. And you are?" he asked.

"Sophia. Now how did you know I was coming tonight?"

Finally, I looked up at him. Absolutely nothing like what I had expected. His hair was hiding one side of his face yes but his eyes; oh, his eyes were so sad.

"I've been dreaming about you for a few weeks now. I didn't know who you were or how I would meet you but today, today I just knew. I knew you would come tonight. Something told me that darkness was the key though so that's why I was sitting here in the dark waiting for you."

And yes, he was cute.

"Please, sit down," he said.

He motioned towards the couch I had stupidly fallen into and sat down across from me.

"So tell me who you are, why you are here and please tell me how you got in my closet."

He looked into my eyes and the butterflies in my stomach had no choice but to flutter. Maybe flutter was an understatement. They were creating a riot in there. I could see them now, looting and starting fires. Okay, well maybe butterflies don't start fires. All right Sophia, calm down, breathe.

"My name is Sophia Elisabeth Winters. I am here to offer you a choice of staying on this realm or joining me on another realm. I ended up in your closet by Reflectioning."

I couldn't help but stare at him. His eyes kept capturing mine and for a moment, I felt lost in them - the color of golden honey.

"Good. Now that you answered all of my questions, can you explain what it all means?"

I really didn't want to do my job. He mesmerized me. Why was he affecting me so much? What exactly was going on here?

"Can I have a glass of water please?" I asked.

He just sat there for a moment looking confused, seemed to snap out of it and hopped up and into the kitchen. A few moments later, he arrived with water. I don't really like water. Can't really keep it down. But I had wanted to distract him, or distract myself from gazing into his eyes and getting lost in there.

"Sorry, I really don't know what to do here. In my dreams, I didn't see you drinking water.

I saw you drinking something…else."

Oh no! Finally, it sunk in and hit me. Precognitive. Can see the future. He saw me in his dreams.

"I really want to know why you are here and why you chose me but for some reason I kind of don't care."

We looked at each other and just laughed. This was actually going to be okay.

"Jeremy, the reason you were chosen is mainly because of your precognitive gift. You could be a valuable asset to the corporation I work for."

He looked so sad. I just wanted to reach over to him and take the sadness away.

"Oh, because of my gift. Is that what you call it?" he snapped.

No. This was not going down the right path.

"Yes, it is a gift if you allow it to be. You can make of it what you want."

He looked up at me and gave me a small smile.

"So if you could see the future you would consider that a gift huh?" he asked.

"If you, for example, are twelve years old and see your parents die in a car accident before it happens and try as hard as you can to prevent it and fail, would you still see it as a gift? What good is seeing the future, good or bad, if you can't ever seem to make things right?"

The sadness of it all was unbearable.

"Jeremy, come with me and join us. Once you are one of us, you will learn to use your powers the way they were meant for you to use them."

He didn't seem convinced.

"What exactly are you?" he asked. Enter my recruiting speech.

"I am a descendant from a very old line of Flesh Cravers and we are zombies to a certain degree. There are many different types of Flesh

Cravers, good and bad. I work for a corporation that the good guys created to try to keep order and peace within our kind. We open our world to anyone who wishes to live there but ask that they help contribute to the peaceful way of life."

Boring. I sounded like a broken record.

"Okay, explain to me what a Flesh Craver is" he said.

Another cue card moment.

"A Flesh Craver is, I mean, I am just like you only with a different diet and extremely hard to kill. Nearly impossible to kill actually. Our diet consists of primarily human flesh. Once you become a Flesh Craver, your body tells you when you need to go on a collection and what exactly you need to collect."

He studied the look on my face.

"Hmm. I don't know what to say. That sounds really cool and all and somewhat gross but I mean, that is kind of a big decision to make. Can you tell me why YOU became one?"

I sighed. A big part of me wanted to tell him to just say no. To tell me to leave and forget I ever existed. I wanted to tell him that I wanted nothing more than to be like him. I wanted to live on his realm and experience his world. I couldn't even spit out that this was not my choice. I guess the long pause answered his question because his next question kind of threw me off guard.

"Okay so don't answer that. But tell me this - I know why I am hating the world right now but tell me Sophia, if you are so happy in your world why do you have the same look of sadness and hopelessness as I feel?"

Those words struck me like lightning and I felt like I would cry.

I wanted to cry because he was right. No, I was not satisfied living my life as a Flesh Craver. No, I was not happy. Yes, I felt sadness almost every day. But how could he possibly see that in a matter of 20 minutes?

"I don't know what you are talking about. I am not sad or hopeless. If you join us you will know exactly what I mean."

This was getting a little too personal and it had to end. Now.

"Listen Jeremy, we don't have much time. I have to get back to my world. Do you want in or not?"

I got up and started pacing around the room. I was avoiding eye contact. Very intuitive this Jeremy guy.

"Can I have a few days to think about it?" he asked.

"No. It is now or never. You only get one invite. If you choose no, you will sleep and when you wake up you will remember none of it, not even your visions of me. If you do come along, we will travel to the city of The Lost Petals and you will begin your training towards your transition."

He turned away and looked into his bedroom.

"Excuse me for a moment" he said, got up and walked away. What was he doing?

I took the opportunity to look around the tiny apartment and something captured my eye. It was the corner of a painting. I got up, walked over to the table, and uncovered the painting. It was a painting of me.

Me, in my blue jeans and white sweater with blue stripes. Me, with my brown hair and black rimmed glasses.

"I see you found my artwork. Do you like it?" he asked.

I swung around because he scared the crap out of me.

"Wow, you did that?" I asked, showing way too much surprise than I really wanted to.

"Yeah I guess I did. When I first dreamt of you, I couldn't get you out of my mind. I had to get your image out of my head or else I was going to go crazy, so I painted you. It really didn't help much but at least I could look at your painting and look at you, not just look at you in my dreams."

I didn't know if I should feel flattered or creeped out.

"Before I make my decision I want to know one thing. Can I take my girl with me?"

Of course, how could I think he was single? And of course, he would want to bring her along. So many others had such a difficult time leaving their loved ones behind.

"No you can't bring your girlfriend along. She was not chosen; you were."

I think I sounded a little too disappointed with a hint of jealousy maybe because he just laughed and I finally got to see what I think was a smile.

"I didn't say my girlfriend, I said my girl. Sophia, meet Munchkin. Munchkin, Sophia."

He moved out of the way and a beautiful cat with stunning blue eyes waltzed over to me like royalty.

"Mow" she said. I think I blushed.

"Well hello kitty. Aren't you just beautiful?"

She looked up at me with those deep blue eyes and her purrs got louder.

"I think she likes you," said Jeremy.

"So, can I take her with me?"

I didn't know what to say. Not many humans

wanted to bring their pet with them, well not when I have recruited them. There were no rules against this, and I think he knew that exact moment I realized he would be coming with me because I smiled and blushed at the same time. "Yes she can come," I said.

"Great. I didn't really want to have to choose you or her. It's nice that I can have you both," he said and I swear he smiled as he said it.

"So, when do we leave?"

Dear Diary,

I met my recruit lead today (Jeremy) and he took the offer. I think I am kind of happy he did. What is with my reaction to him though? He made me feel all funny inside as if he knew me down to my soul.

When we Reflectioned to The Lost Petals, the images I saw from his mind were so heartbreaking. I saw a demolished car, which could only be his parents' car accident and I saw him as a young child in a corner, crying. I also saw him as a young teen in a foster home and then he moved into a foster home where his foster parents were alcoholics.

It was only a three-second trip, but when we got back to my cubicle, I realized I had been crying. Jeremy told me it was all right and that the hurt has mostly dissipated, but I don't believe him. I mean, I can see the pain in his eyes.

I don't know. From the moment I laid eyes on him, he captured me. Me. Strong willed, complicated, stubborn me. I called Cecily when I got home and told her a little about Jeremy. She immediately said "ohh you've got it bad for him." Cecily is such a pain I don't know what to do with her sometimes.

I had introduced Jeremy to Evan and Evan took him into his office to get the paperwork started. Jeremy asked if I could look after Munchkin for him since he didn't want to move her too much. "She might get stressed," he had said. When he said that, he looked at her with so much love and adoration. He loved his cat.

It was then and there that I realized that he could love with no boundaries. That no matter what happened in his life, no matter how much pain he was in, he could still find that part of him that could love freely.

Maybe it was too soon to feel this way but it was one of those things that I could not control and I think I didn't want to control it. From the second I saw him, he left me weak and speechless.

Before I left work today, Jeremy came out of Evans' office and rushed over to my cubicle. He thanked me for taking care of Munchkin and told me he was very happy I came looking for him. Munchkin had settled on my desk with her tail neatly tucked under her.

While I had been working, she gazed at me every so often with her diamond blue eyes and I knew she was special. I had never really considered cats before. They just seemed like irritating earthly creatures. Lazy - only wanting love on their terms, and that absolutely gross and disgusting part about cleaning litter boxes. So not my thing. But, Munchkin, I could definitely see myself sharing my apartment with such a fascinating, beautiful creature.

Evan was talking to Shelley, another recruiter, when Jeremy leaned into me to ask me a question.

"Sophia, when we were traveling through that mirror world I know you saw my parents' car accident and how horrified I was. But tell me something. Who were the two Angels?"

Going to bed now since I'm agitated. I never did answer him.

4 THE FIRST DAY

So okay, getting up this morning was just plain cruel. I had been thinking and dreaming about Jeremy all night. Seriously, was I going to turn into one of those crazies who could not live without that one special person? Think about something else. Shower - must get a shower. So, I went into the bathroom to run the shower, and why did I get so many freakin' visitors?

"Hi Melody. What are you doing here so early in the day?" I asked.

"I just popped in to say hi Sophia. We haven't been able to catch up in a while."

Melody is a Mist Fairy and can only appear when steam or fog is around. Makes it very difficult to keep friendships that way.

"I really can't talk for long - getting ready to go to work. Maybe we can make a date this weekend?"

I was so not in the mood to talk. I wanted to get my shower and start my day.

"It's okay Sophia. You don't have to promise something you won't do. Just tell me you don't want to be friends anymore and I'll stop coming around."

Damn it all to hell. It's hard to see her facial expression what with all the steam but it was easy to hear in her voice she was upset.

"I'm sorry I haven't been keeping my promises Melody and of course I want to be friends. It's just that it's been so crazy at work that I really don't have the time to do much of anything else. I REALLY PROMISE we can do something this weekend. How about a movie?"

She floated around me like a shark circling its prey and swooped directly in front of my face, kind of startling me.

"Really Sophia? You'll go to all the trouble for us to watch a movie?"

She was so excited I couldn't say no.

"Of course. You are one of my best friends Melody. What's a little conjuring for friends?"

She continued to float around me in circles and it was making me somewhat dizzy.

"But I don't want you to get hurt again" she said and the disappointment in her voice was overwhelming.

"I will be prepared this time so that I DON'T get hurt."

She clapped her misty hands together and gave me a big hug. Of course, I could not feel anything because her form is created by the mist and she just sort of floated through me.

"Thank you Sophia. You are the bestest friend anyone could ever have. See you this weekend" and she was gone.

I really do like Melody, but she can get a little needy sometimes.

I showered and got a cup of coffee. I know it makes me really sick to my stomach, but dammit, I wanted coffee. I would deal with the stomach cramps later. Since natural Flesh Cravers don't turn until the great old age of eighteen, I did enjoy the finer things in human life. One of those things was coffee.

Mocha raspberry iced coffee with extra cream and extra sugar. Oh, I will so pay for this.

On my way to the office, I picked up the newspaper and lo and behold, Old Lady Mamie was at it again. It read:

CROP CIRCLES PROVE THEY WERE HERE says Old Lady Mamie.

That woman really needs some friends.

Up the steps and into the elevator. As I stepped out of the elevator, I walked right into Sam. Oh joy.

"Hi Sam, how's it going?" I asked.

"Fine. Fine. I was just thinking about you. I heard about what Henderson did to you with that newly turned girl Chloe. What a shitty thing really. How can he be so irresponsible?"

He said the last sentence with such disgust I had to stifle a laugh. He hated Henderson. With a passion. But he hated him for reasons only Sam could hate him for. He hated him because he was tall. He hated him because he was popular. He hated him the most because he took every opportunity to hit on me on a daily basis.

Not just hit on me, but also vulgar, crude, extremely inappropriate comments frequently spewed from his mouth. Henderson's sexual innuendos were endless.

"I don't know what that man thinks most of the time. I try to avoid him whenever possible," I said.

"You just make sure you stay away from him," he said.

"I don't trust him. His scent is all wrong."

So Sam is a Scenter. He has this ability to smell things about a person. He can smell fear. He can smell love. He can smell hatred. He can smell evil. More often than not, he tells me to stay away from Henderson. He also tells me to stay away from anyone who may want to ask me out on a date.

"Don't worry Sam. I will be glad to stay away from him."

I walked away so that he could just shut up. I was starting to see his jealousy ooze out of his pores and I really didn't want to get into that. Not now. I had other plans for today. I just thank every higher being that he couldn't smell my lies or my repulsion towards him.

As I turned from Sam, I spotted Jeremy coming out of the elevator. He was wearing khaki pants with a red t-shirt. His hair was loose and caressed his shoulders with a little strand straying away from the rest of the group and hanging over his eye.

He looked like a dream. Red was most definitely his color. As he walked towards me, I quickly opened up my purse and pretended to be looking for something so that I wasn't so obviously desperate to see him.

He saw me right away and he walked faster in my direction.

"Hey Sophia. How are you doing today?"

I continued to rummage through my purse and became so frantic I dropped it - everything spilled out. Just great.

"Here, I'll help you" he said. At the same exact moment we bent down to gather my crap, we bumped heads so hard I saw stars. We both fell over and looked at each other with surprise.

"We really have to stop meeting this way," he said.

At that, we laughed and he helped me up.

"What do you say we get out of here and get some fresh air?" he said.

I was still disoriented by the bump. However, I managed to mumble a quick "okay".

"Where can I get some food around here?" he said.

"We can go to the diner down the street. They have all kinds of different foods for many different species and beings."

I finally got all of my stuff back into my purse and patted down my clothes. Why was I so nervous? This was crazy!

"Do you mind if we make a quick trip to my apartment before we go? I have to feed Munchkin. If I don't feed her at exactly the same time every day she takes it personally."

I giggled at this. I could just see Munchkin, taking it personally and doing something like quickly turning away from him in anger.

"Sure, that sounds like a plan," I said.

This is where Jeremy surprised me for the first time and took my hand in his.

"Is this ok?" he asked. Oh my Goddess oh my Goddess oh my Goddess. YES. YES, of course it is okay. I tried to catch my breath before I answered him but I think he could hear me breathing. I think the entire office could hear me breathing.

"Yeah, that's okay" I finally mumbled.

We walked over to the elevator and entered together. We were immediately transported to the 115th floor - the New Recruit Lead floor. This is where we set up our newbies for their first year or so until they get the hang of the change and can live on their own without killing everyone and everything in their path.

As we walked down the hall, Jeremy continued to hold my hand in his. I swear he felt my heart racing in my hand. We got to his apartment door and he let go. I looked up at him not wanting him to let go and wondering why he did, but he didn't notice. He was getting his key card out from his wallet. Oh no - I WAS becoming needy. Why? I have met so many guys throughout my life. Why this one? What makes him so special?

Entering his apartment, I was instantly drawn to the dining room table. On it were little tubs of magnificent colors, paintbrushes, sketches, small paintings, and small drawings - his artwork! He saw me glance that way and walked over to it.

"It's not Picasso but I like to think I do a pretty decent job."

He raised his hand to his hair and tucked the foolish strands behind his ear. Yes, totally sexy. I think I stopped breathing.

"I'll just be a minute" he said and walked into the kitchen.

As I looked through his artwork, I stumbled across a sketchbook in which most of the pages had some type of sketch, some type of drawing. I opened it to the first page, and with horror, I couldn't help but continue turning the pages. Page one sketch displayed the same mutilated car we saw in Reflection World. Page two displayed Jeremy as a young child, sobbing on a sidewalk.

Page three displayed a bottle of whiskey with blood dripping from the bottom. I was trying extremely hard not to cry. Why was Jeremy finding it so hard to let go of his hurtful past? Maybe I could help him with that.

Being a Flesh Craver and living essentially

forever allows us many years of practice losing loved ones. You eventually learn to live alone. Not the ideal life but you never know when you will meet that special someone that could live for eternity with you.

"Find anything you like?" asked Jeremy from directly behind me.

I jumped at his voice and dropped the sketchbook onto the floor.

"I'm so sorry; here let me get that" I said.

This time, he let me rush down to pick up the book.

"Oh, sorry Sophia. I really wish you hadn't seen all of that."

This sadness in Jeremy was contagious. All of his sorrow and hurt feelings seemed to pass over to me and overwhelm me in a rush of despondency.

"Jeremy I'm so sorry. I didn't mean to intrude..."

He didn't let me finish my thought, just put his fingertip against my lips and said "don't apologize. It is because of you that I am able to hopefully start a new life and leave the old one behind." His hand slowly moved over to my cheek and we gazed into each other's eyes. He was going to kiss me. I was SO not complaining.

At that moment, Jeremy raised his hands to his temples and let out a howl. He collapsed onto the floor and lay there staring up at the ceiling.

"Jeremy! Jeremy, are you okay?" I asked and now I was starting to panic.

Not only was I panicking because Jeremy seemed to be having some sort of seizure, I was panicking because I realized I was hungry and when he put his fingertip upon my lips, I wanted to bite.

I sat on the floor next to Jeremy while he lay there. He had a nosebleed about five minutes into the attack. I ran to the kitchen and grabbed a dishtowel to slow the bleeding. I put his head on my lap and rocked him back and forth.

He was still breathing but he continued to stare into nowhere. This maybe lasted for about fifteen minutes, and then Jeremy closed his eyes and fell asleep. I lay down next to him and lay with him the entire time.

I don't really know how long we were laying there on the floor but at some point I fell asleep too. When I woke up, Jeremy had draped one arm across my chest and had his face in my neck. He was still asleep. His breathing was tickling my neck. My breathing was making his arm go up and down, up and down, up and down.

I thought for sure the accelerated pace of my breathing would wake him from his sound sleep. I felt something heavy on my leg and realized that Munchkin joined us in our slumber. What time was it?

"Jeremy, are you awake?" I asked.

He mumbled something I couldn't understand and I felt his eyelashes against my ear causing a weird tickle that wasn't quite ticklish.

Jeremy shot up from the floor and nearly took my head with him.

"I am so sorry Sophia are you alright? I can't believe this happened with you. Did I hurt you?"

He sat on the couch and put his head in his hands, elbows on his thighs. He seemed out of it, but otherwise, okay.

"Yes I am okay. It's not me you have to

worry about. What the hell was that? Are YOU okay?" I asked.

I picked Munchkin up off my leg and carried her over to the couch where Jeremy was. She quickly jumped to the back of the couch directly behind him and walked onto his shoulder, settling herself behind the crook of his neck.

"That was one of my visions," he said.

"That is what you call my gift. I'll be right back."

He got up (yes Munchkin was still on his shoulder) and went to the bathroom. He came out of the bathroom, walked into the kitchen and grabbed a glass of water. His hair had fallen over his face again. He put two pills into his mouth and washed them down with the water.

So now what? I didn't know quite what to do or what to say. If all of his visions were like this, how COULD we call it a gift? It looked painful as hell! What if this were to happen out on the street? What if this were to happen while you were driving? The dangerous possibilities were endless.

"Sophia listen, you don't have to stay if you don't want to. I know this is really weird and I was stupid to think you would want to get to know me better."

What? He thought HE was weird. Hello - I'm the one that eats flesh! "Jeremy please come sit with me," I said.

He walked over to the couch and finally put Munchkin down. She was not too pleased and she showed it by latching onto his shirt with all four sets of claws. He seemed to have some practice as he unlatched each one until she was loose. He sat down next to me and looked down. I inched closer to him and felt him flinch.

What did he see in that vision that made him afraid of me? I took my hand, placed a couple of fingers against his cheek and turned his head until he was facing me. I took my other hand and pulled his hair back behind his ear. "Jeremy, whatever it is you are going through, I will be right here with you every step of the way." With both hands on his face, I finally realized how intimate this was getting. I looked into his eyes and was immediately lost in a mix of emotions. How can someone be so sad yet look at you with such passion?

"Listen Jer…"

I couldn't even get his name out before he leaned in and kissed me. He kissed me with a desire so deep; a passion hidden for so long that when released it came rushing out in a series of tidal waves. Jeremy put his hands on my cheeks and pulled me closer to him. I was so NOT complaining. I embraced his neck and we pulled each other in so tight there is no way we could have gotten any closer.

Wait Sophia! What the hell are you doing? I am so crossing some serious recruiter boundaries here. I pulled back and slid away from him, certainly not wanting to, but feeling I had to.

"What's wrong?" he asked. "Did I do something wrong?"

"You most certainly didn't do anything wrong Jeremy but I think that maybe we need to focus a little here. I am your recruiter. It is not ideal for a recruiter and a recruit lead to become involved…...romantically."

Okay, so I know I led him on and I know

what you are thinking. Shut up Sophia and for once let your heart guide you. Was this me or Cecily talking in my head?

"I don't know who made the rules up but they stink. I will do whatever you want me to do Sophia. Just say the words."

Jeremy looked at me and captured me with his eyes once again. He so needed to stop doing that. I don't know when it was that I started losing my self-control when I was around him, but I didn't like it one bit. Jeremy had totally won me over. He didn't even DO anything!

"Let's take this one step at a time Jeremy. First, we need to go get some food. Second, we need to talk about your plans. The rest we can figure out as we go."

I got up to prove to him that I could move and we should get going but my legs gave me away and I stumbled a little. He got up and caught me and now I was in his arms. Great. Just great. Sophia, whatever you do, don't look into his eyes. Don't look into his eyes.

"Sophia, if we are going to be spending a lot of time together you have to know one other thing about me."

Oh great. This was it. I knew there was something about him I needed to know.

"Sure, what is that Jeremy?" I asked. He was still holding me in his arms and looking down at me. He said softly,

"I have been waiting for you for a very long time, and I'm not going let you go so easily."

With that tiny, romantic tidbit, he kissed me again. Oh hell. I let him.

Dear Diary,

Okay, so maybe I didn't make the best decisions today. After we left Jeremy's apartment, we went to the diner. I excused myself for a minute or two, went into the bathroom and went on a quick collection.

I hadn't eaten in a few days and I really didn't want to hurt Jeremy. Plus, I noticed a little rash on my leg and that was the beginning sign that decomposition was starting to set in. Some of my skin has begun to peel up.

The yellows and blues had started to peek their way through to the surface of my skin, and my flesh was beginning to ooze. I know that will never be not gross. My meal consisted of fresh cheekbone flesh – chewy on the outside and warm gooey deliciousness on the inside. I was trying to hurry to get back to Jeremy, and was a bit sloppy with collection this time around and managed to get blood all over me.

When I got back, Jeremy had ordered a breakfast platter with the works - scrambled eggs, bacon, sausage, hash browns, pancakes and orange juice. He looked up at me, looked at my shirt, started to say something, and I suppose he was at a loss for words. He did grow a little paler though. I looked at his meal with the eggs all runny and the bacon all greasy - I thought I would be sick.

I ordered a glass of water. I had thought of ordering a glass of something more my style, but he looked like he was going to blow chunks all over his breakfast so I decided I had better stick to my glass of water that I wouldn't even drink.

We made small talk. The diner I brought Jeremy to was called Eats and Treats. Jeremy browsed the menu. After he had gotten past his nausea, he had fun asking me all sorts of questions regarding the menu.

Appetizers ranged from Greemor toes and Ladelieon excrement to mozzarella sticks and potato wedges. Jeremy chuckled as he continued to read on the lunch specials: roasted ogre tongue topped with fresh troll saliva and chives. Chives!

After brunch, we went back to the office and I continued my day while he continued his orientation. Time doesn't matter here. We pretty much do what we need to do when we need to do it. I don't know, it just works out that way.

Before Jeremy went back to orientation, however, he said one last thing to me with a quirky grin on his face: "you have a little blood on your chin" and he wiped it away with his finger. He left me sitting there, embarrassed to the nth degree (and why didn't he tell me I had that the entire time we were at brunch?!). Through it all, I thought to myself "wow, that was so romantic." Ok. Gag me. I am really pathetic here.

So anyway, after he left, I finished up my work and went over to Cecily's where I became horribly ill (the coffee finally caught up with me) and I threw up the entire night. Glomulis everywhere. After my failed attempt at cleaning up (Cecily said she would take care of it, thank Goddess Hiliad), I was able to Reflection myself home, barely, got a shower and lay in bed. Now I was thinking about Jeremy. I wondered what he was doing. I wondered what he was thinking. I wondered if he was thinking of me. I needed to stop thinking and go to bed. Until next time dear diary…

5 EXPLANATIONS

So today I vowed to not fall all over Jeremy. It was Friday and I could make it through the day. Come on Sophia. Be strong. Be cool. Be calm. I made my way through the crowd towards F.L.E.S.H., mumbling my new mantra and looking at my feet as I walked. No sense in running into someone and try to make chit chat when all I wanted to do was be home under the covers, asleep (secretly dreaming of Jeremy). Stop it Soph!

I stepped off the elevator and skittered over to my cubicle. Hopefully no one had seen me. I can just get my paperwork done, avoid anyone and everyone and go home. Easy right? Well, it would be easy if I were not me.

"Hey Sophia" said Sam as he plopped himself down on the chair in front of my desk.

"So, I really need to talk to you and I think you should listen. Is that okay?"

Oh no. Why now Sam? Any other time but now! I really did not want to do this now! "Sam, I am kinda bus-"

"NO! You just need to not interrupt me and listen. Stay away from Jeremy! He smells funny. I cannot exactly pinpoint what it is but he is not right. I am not saying this because I do not want you to be happy. I am saying this because I love you."

There it was. Finally the confession of love. I knew he cared about me, but I did not think it was love.

"Sam, what do you mean he smells funny? You are the expert on "Scenting." You should know what it means, right?"

He looked at me, and sweet mother of Hiliad I think he was about to pop a blood vessel. The little veins on his temples were jutting out and the big vein on the side of his neck was turning purple. His face turned beet red, and the acne on his face was turning all of the imaginable shades of red and pink you can think up.

"SOPHIA did you hear what I just said? I said I love you. Do you have anything you would like to say about that? Can you tell me how you feel about that? Are you really as coldhearted as everyone says you are?"

With that, he got up and walked away. Before he left though, he poked his head in one last time and said,

"Even if you don't love me too, I still don't want to see you get hurt. Please don't continue this thing you have with Jeremy."

He stormed off like a child sent to his room for bad behavior.

Well great. Now that Sam was mad at me, I guess I couldn't go ask him a little more about Scenting. I suppose it is never a bad day to go to the library.

Sure, I could say a spell and have a book appear on my desk. Sure I could even look this up on the web (we have our own search engine zzz.flesh.zom). But, I like to do things on my own. I walked over to the elevator and decided what the hell. Let me take the stairs. The library is only three floors down. I could definitely use the walk to clear my head a bit after my encounter with Sam.

I made my way down the steps and realized just how creepy the halls really were. Hardly anyone used the stairs, so they don't really take care of them very well. Very little lighting and dark walls make for a great horror movie. I should know. I love them. I live them.

Down the first flight, I came across an ogre. So okay, an ogre can come in all different shapes and sizes. They have jobs to do and don't like being bothered while they are doing them. This must be the stairwell janitor ogre.

This particular ogre was about one foot tall and had ears that hung down its body all the way to the floor. They had mouths filled with razor sharp teeth so you had better be careful when dealing with them.

As I stepped over him, he yelled at me "Hey watch it lady. Just because you don't have this job doesn't mean you have to ruin all of my hard work!" and he had the nerve to hit me with his miniature mop. And wow, did that hurt!

"Sorry, I am just passing through," I said as I stepped over him. He held out his mop and waved it at my legs again.

"STAY OFF OF MY STAIRS" he yelled. I quickly ran down the steps and into the hallway. Sheesh, what a little stinker.

Entering the library of F.L.E.S.H. is truly a spectacular experience. The library staff consisting of Knowledge Fairies welcome you. They flutter around the library, tidying up and helping patrons find what they are looking for. There are males and females, however, they all have long flowing hair. Their wings are so quiet and flutter so fast you barely see them. Their complexions have a pinkish hue to them making them look like they have too much blush on.

Their voices are barely whispers, but you can hear them perfectly.

"Welcome to the Department of Literary Works and Other Texts of Knowledge. We are so happy you have come to visit. Is there anything we may be able to assist you with?" They always speak in the "we and us" sense. Knowledge Fairies share one collective core. They think the same, they learn the same, and they even sound the same.

"I'm doing a little research on Scenting and wanted to find the best book out there that can help me study it."

One of the fairies smiled and zipped away into the shelves. She came back almost immediately with a book in her hands.

"We believe this is what you are looking for. Please sign out at the front desk. Have a wonderful day," she said and just like that, the fairies were off helping other patrons that had walked in.

Okay, so it's not like I found the book myself but this is still better than going online and cheating. Yes, I consider it cheating. Looks like I was going back to my cubicle to do a little reading. This time, I would be taking the elevator, thank you very much.

Stepping off the elevator and rushing to my cubicle seemed like a great idea however, luck was not on my side.

"Sophia! Sophia! Look at me!"

I heard a shrill, shrieky voice yell out my name and wow, did I want her to shut up before my eardrums burst.

"Chloe hey how are you? You look so much better. Your head is intact again," I said.

She smiled and touched the side of her head that was missing before.

"Sophia it was so cool. After we got back and you handed me off to Summer, she took me upstairs and I learned so much. Did you know that when we go on collections we can actually feel what part of the body we have to bite to satisfy the hunger? It's like images form in your head and you just know!"

"Oh, oh, and did you know that when you recite the sleep retention spell it not only makes the potential victim sleep like he is dead, but it affects everyone within the surrounding mile radius? If they are not asleep, they will continue what they are doing but just not remember what it was they did."

"Oh, oh, and when the victim wakes up, they don't even feel any pain where we fed. For example, if we take an ear off, the victim will wake up with the wound stitched up and they will actually remember being in some sort of accident that totally explains everything. AND this spell also puts these false memories into other peoples' minds so that they can confirm the accident."

"Oh, oh, and I finally got my necklace Sophia! I got my Flesh Craver necklace. I went on my own collection and sealed my fate! I am so excited!"

Oh my Goddess Chloe shut UP! She was giddy and giggling and I swear she was humming with happiness. The happiness oozed from her. I would have preferred her with half of a head at this point in time.

"Chloe that's great. I am so glad that Summer introduced you to your bible. Make sure you study it completely and routinely. It will prove to be a very valuable resource."

She hopped over to me and gave me a huge hug.

"Thank you so much Sophia! Without you I never would have made it this far. My experience with you in Reflection World gave me the courage to give it a try. I will never forget your help."

She gave me a quick kiss on the cheek and was in the elevator before I could say you're welcome.

In my cubicle, I found a bouquet of flowers on my desk. There was a little note on it with some scribbling.

Thank you for accepting me. Hope to see you soon, Jeremy

There went the butterflies.

There went the lump in my throat.

There went my mantra right out the window.

Okay, he got me. He got me good. What do I do now?

"So, got a secret admirer there Sophia?"

Oh no, Evan. I so cannot tell him who these are from.

"Oh yeah, you know, the usual mystery bouquet of flowers." Please don't ask, please don't ask.

"Must be nice to be liked so much. Let me know when I get to meet this fella."

Just like that, he walked away. Whew! So close! Now let me put these flowers away before anyone else noticed them. Finally, I can read my book.

Chapter 1: History of Scenting

Scenters are direct descendants of the canine species. No, they are not dogs or werewolves (although werewolves do exist). They are descendants of the canine species due to a research scientist that studied canines and their many senses.

Dr. Bandar Kane discovered that a dog has over 220 million scent receptors compared to a humans' 2 million. Years of laboratory experiments allowed Dr. Kane to isolate the DNA to those receptors and implant them into human beings. Throughout these experiments, Dr. Kane studied multiple subjects at multiple stages of the implant. Some patients were only given two receptors at a time - for example, the scents of rain and sunlight. These scents proved to be valuable in that the subjects could tell Dr. Kane when it was going to rain (usually the subjects were about two hours off) and when the next sunrise would occur.

In some subjects, Dr. Kane implanted tornado and hurricane scent receptors. These proved to be beneficial. However, the subjects complained of constant headaches and migraines. They also developed tumors and cysts in the brain within five years of the implant leading to instant death. Dr. Kane has denied that these claims had any correlation to the implants.

"Wow, this is really fascinating. Yawn. Let me skip a few chapters."

Chapter 8: Scenting Delays and Responses

You will encounter some occasions in which you are not able to identify a certain scent. This could be for a number of reasons, although the most popular reason is change. The world continues to change and with changes in atmosphere, breeding, and even death will come foreign scents. Do not give up, as your body just needs a little time to adjust to the new scents. Be sure to expose yourself to these scents as often as possible to give your scent receptors the opportunity to detect and study them. If after continuous exposure to the foreign scent provides no results, please consult your scent physician as you may have an infection in your receptors, which requires immediate medical care...

"A-ha!" It's not Jeremy that's the problem, it's Sam.

I knew it. That little scumbag. He is just trying to scare me into thinking that there is something wrong with Jeremy just so that I don't get to know him better. I don't know why I even bothered listening to Sam in the first place.

I should have known his motives were purely selfish. Feeling satisfied, I tossed the book into my desk drawer and made a mental note to return it to the library before I left work. Now I should actually try to get some work done.

In my inbox, there were twenty recruit-lead case files. Sigh. Seriously, are there that many leads in this world? And, am I the only recruiter here?

The problem with my job is that we do not only go to the human realm to recruit. Nope - we travel to all sorts of realms. I once went to The Realm of Flames and tried to get a fire demon to join us, and whoa was she nasty. Not only did she kick my ass, she tore a hole into me so big that it took a month for me to heal. She obviously did not want to join us.

Apparently, fire demons can shoot fire from their fingertips. This particular fire demon shot me smack on the thigh. I was in bed for a couple of weeks before I could walk again. Evan had visited me every day apologizing for sending me out on that case. I still brought it up at very convenient times so that I could hopefully get out of a case I really didn't want to work on. Sometimes it worked, sometimes it didn't.

On another case, I went to the Shadow Empire. This place is SUPER EERIE! The only inhabitants of the Shadow Empire are the souls of those who performed unforgivable acts of violence and they are just shadows, silhouettes. I am not sure who makes up the rules, but their acts must be pretty bad to get them to land here.

Anyway, there was a shadow soul named Solhava that had the gift of possession and I was sent to recruit him before our enemies did. He came along but three months into his lessons, he was taken by the Aegrurian Corporation (this is one of the groups of the not so good Flesh Cravers that want to take over the underworld).

They kidnapped Solhava and I have no idea how they held him hostage but eventually Solhava took to their views and I occasionally hear of him possessing someone into joining the Aegrurians. As you can see, some adventures are fun while others are downright nasty.

As I sifted through my new case files I came across one of a little girl. Damn. I was so hesitant to recruit children only because I didn't think it was fair to make a child make this kind of a decision. Sometimes it ends badly. Let's see what her case file has to say.

6 BUT SHE'S ONLY A CHILD

Case file of Netasha Rolette

Full Name: Netasha Rolette
Address: 92138 Silver Dwelling Road Dallas TX 75211
Phone Number: 972-661-7327
DOB: 8/23
Height: 4'10 Weight: 115 lbs
Occupation: Student/high school drop out, age 15
Medical History: Hospitalized at the age of 6 for hallucinations and self inflicted injuries.
Medications: Geodon - Antipsychotic - 20mg 2x/day
Family History: Parents abandoned Netasha once she was admitted into the psychiatric ward. Their whereabouts are unknown. No record of siblings or relatives.
Mental Health: Claims to see, hear and speak to the dead.
Lead Information: Netasha ran away from the hospital and is hiding out in abandoned buildings. Current age is 15. She has one month's supply of medication with her. Daily monitoring has identified Netasha frequently speaks to unseen entities and routinely awakens in the middle of the night with nightmares. She also acquires injuries of unknown origin. She is isolated from society and seems to

prefer being alone.
Daily Itinerary: Shoplifts food and clothing to survive.
Pets: none

Oh no. Maybe I had better get to her soon. She is only a little kid! I set aside all of the other case files because well, I didn't want to be distracted. I needed to get to this girl quickly before she hurt herself!

I walked over to my mirror and just as I was going to whisper my Reflectioning spell, Jeremy entered my cubicle. I stopped breathing and seriously forgot what I was doing.

"Can I come along with you?" he asked.

Dammit! I never take anyone on my travels for recruit leads. It's kind of my own personal rule - never take someone along to distract you of your responsibilities.

"Uh Jeremy, I don't usually have company on the job. I mean how would you have felt if I had shown up with someone else when I came to get you?"

He didn't seem convinced and just smiled at me. He knew he was going to get to me and whatever I said would just be, well, a lie.

"C'mon. You need backup. What if this recruit lead is all dangerous and tries to hurt you?" he said.

He looked at me with those sad lonely eyes and really, as much as I wanted to say no, I didn't have the heart. I think he is a hazard to my job.

"Okay you can come but here's the deal. You do NOT under ANY circumstances try to intervene here. She is MY recruit lead. It is MY responsibility to convince her she wants to join us. Do you have any questions?" I asked.

I didn't think he would so I quickly said

"give me your hand and we will travel together. Don't think you can make it there on your own without getting lost." And at this, I smiled. Ah, it was good to have the upper hand at SOMETHING with Jeremy.

"Great. I don't have any questions now but can I ask you the questions as they come up?" he asked.

"Only if they don't interfere with the recruiting then yes."

I think that upset him a little but I couldn't really tell because although he smiled a lot lately, his eyes still told the story of a lonely sad man looking for something. I wished I knew what that was.

"Okay let's go."

We entered Reflection World and hello Max and beautiful Angel wife. I really wished I would just stop seeing him already. We zipped past the car accident, exited Reflection World and ended up in a dark, damp warehouse of some kind. No lights and lots of random noises (skittering noises thank you very much! I loathe rodents with a passion!).

Jeremy was still holding my hand and I think I was still not breathing. It's just that whenever he touched me I felt a tingle that started at the point where he touched me and traveled throughout my entire body. Very hard to explain, so I won't continue trying.

"Where ARE we?" Jeremy asked.

"This place is really creepy. I know I am not a Flesh Craver yet but seriously, do you ever get to the point where none of this scares you?"

I wanted to say yes, but so could not.

"Well, depending on who you are and how you work, you could get rid of those fears because you KNOW you are very much difficult to kill. However if you are anything like me, you will keep those fears and sometimes they get worse!"

He laughed at me (seemed like the thing to do nowadays) and said, "you really are too much!"

Okay. Well, moving on.

"We are looking for Netasha. Stop talking and focus," I said.

Oh well, I was being harsh. So what? I really did not want to get into small talk but at the same time I DID tell him I would be here for him no matter what - after all I AM his recruiter. That's exactly it. I AM his recruiter and the feelings I have for him (and I hope he has for me) are a no-no. I mean, there is no rule or anything like that but it's just something that's frowned upon.

Oh alright so the real reason it's frowned upon since I know you will eventually ask is because this recruiter a long time ago fell in love with his recruit lead. He found his lead almost at the point of death (suicide) because the lead couldn't handle their "gift" any longer. Apparently the gift was she was an empath (feel what other people around them are feeling).

She became so wrapped up in everyone else's feelings and trying to comfort them, that she was not acknowledging the things that were bothering her. She was not realizing that she too was hurting and needed help - she did not help herself.

She got to the point where all she was feeling was the pain of others and she could no longer handle it. She was too stubborn to address the fact that allowing these feelings to completely engulf her every being was dangerous, lethal to empaths.

The recruiter found her having taken multiple pills in an attempt to take her own life. When he got to her, she thought he was a hallucination but he took her in and helped her heal.

Two weeks after she came to The Lost Petals she wandered into Pleasers Alley and the feelings of pain overwhelmed her. She had a nervous breakdown and had to be hospitalized. From that day on, she had to be isolated from everyone - she needed to be sedated in order for her to be fed. She could not handle feeling other peoples' feelings. Even the recruiter could not visit her. Even his pain was too much for her.

It only lasted six months but the recruiter could not take it anymore. He loved her and he could not see her. He broke into the F.L.E.S.H. archives, found the reverse forever spell and killed himself. End of story. She is still "alive" and in the hospital (Creshing Center for the Mentally Unstable - yes I know - there's not much to hide there).

Back to now. Jeremy was holding my hand. I think I was finally breathing. Noises of things lurking in the dark. I saw a light up ahead. "Look over there" I whispered.

"I think that's where she is."

As we inched closer, the light got brighter until it almost hurt my eyes. When we walked into the room, Netasha jumped out in front of us with a knife.

"Move one more foot and I will slice out your heart" she said.

Ouch - she is a tough one.

"Netasha hi, I'm Sophia and this is Jeremy.

Please don't hurt us. We are here to help you."

As soon as I said this, she let out an airy laugh, somewhat eerie since little kid laughter totally creeps me out.

"Help me? YOU are here to help ME? That's funny. There is NO WAY I am going back to the hospital and if you so much as try to touch me, you're cut."

"We're not here from the hospital," said Jeremy. "We are here from -"

I jabbed him with my elbow in his side and made him cough a little. What was he doing?

"What did I tell you?" I said. "I do all the talking; you just stand there and do nothing."

He gave me a look like he was angry with me. Finally some emotion other than sadness.

"Fine. I was just trying to help," he said.

Now, I felt guilty. Strike two for me.

"Netasha, if you would please just put the knife down and let us tell you why we are here I would really appreciate it."

She looked me up and down and said, "Okay, you have five minutes. Start talking." So I did.

Overall, it took about four and a half minutes to get her convinced. I think the only reason she agreed to come with us was that she did not know where else to hide and she did not want to go back to the hospital. No matter the reason, I was glad she decided to come along. I was glad we were able to save her.

7 CONFUSION

As we neared the mirror to get back to F.L.E.S.H., Netasha followed behind us, clearly demonstrating she did not trust us. The knife was still out but at least she had the blade facing the floor as she walked.

"So how are we getting there?" she asked.

"We are going to Reflection out of here and into The Lost Petals" I said.

Yes, I know she didn't know what Reflectioning was but she would soon enough. Sometimes I just get tired of explaining.

Jeremy grabbed my hand (which by the way was all sweaty and clammy thank you very much nerves) because I KNEW he would go for my hand again.

"You nervous?" he asked.

Great. Now he can tell when I am nervous.

"No. I am just anxious to get back home. Have some research to do for my next recruit lead."

He looked at me with that look - the one that says 'I know you are lying to me, just tell me the truth.' I couldn't tell him I wanted to do a little more research on him. Damn Sam really got me thinking - why did Jeremy smell "not right" to him?

"Okay, do you want some company or help with the research?" he asked.

And yes I just knew he would ask that.

"Umm sure." I set the trap and I fell into it.

"Oh gross. Just kiss and get a room already you two. Can you be any more obvious?" said Netasha.

I blushed and glared at her.

"Don't know what you are talking about Netasha. You're not making much sense. But then again, you ARE just a kid."

Okay so that was so uncalled for. Hey, I was nervous and she was being a brat.

"Whatever" she said.

"Let's just get to where we need to be so that I don't have to keep hearing you two flirt with each other."

"Myfirio Teithio" and off we were into Reflection World. As we stepped into Reflection World, I was expecting to see more disturbing images of Jeremy's memories of the car accident but instead I saw Jeremy as he was now. He was standing there looking over at me and he looked so sad - I was immediately filled with gloom and distress and I had to look away.

I had to remind myself this was Reflection World and it was most likely to show you false images. Hi Max, hi beautiful and irritating Angel wife. I was really getting tired of seeing him. It's hard to get over someone when you see them EVERY FREAKIN DAY!

Another scene instantly distracted me. This one was very disturbing, but I could not look away. There were two cloaked figures crouched down, huddled over a figure laying on the ground. The background scenery was that of a

cemetery and it was dark. The figures were
making horrible sucking and grunting sounds.
I cleared my throat because all of a sudden my
throat was dry as hell. I was scared. At once
one of the figures looked up at me and I was
petrified beyond words.

It was horrible. Its face was pale, almost
paper white. Its teeth were long and fanglike
with what I would assume to be blood dripping
in globs from them. The figure on the ground was
contorted in a position only gymnasts could PROBABLY
replicate but nonetheless unnatural. I realized that
figure on the ground was Netasha.

At that moment, the crouching figure rushed over to
us and jumped at me. Yes, these images can touch you if
you think they can. I thought they could. It pounced on
me and I was torn from Jeremy's hand. The creature was
disgusting - it had knocked me down to the ground and
was staring me in the face.

I could see it now, up close and personal. It was
like nothing I had ever seen (and I have seen a lot).
As it was looking down at me, its glowing red eyes
seemed to penetrate deep down to my very soul. Viscous
fluids were oozing from its mouth onto my face. Gross!
If I make it out of here in one piece, I am going to
take a nice, long, hot and well deserved bath!

The creature raised a finger to its lips and
whispered "Shh. You will wake the child."

But, it came out more like an airy final
smelly breath. I felt a tug on my arm and I
was pulled towards the mirror, out of
Reflection World and into my office.

"What the hell was that?" asked Jeremy.

I didn't know what to tell him. I didn't
know either! "I don't know. Netasha, what were
they?" I asked. Netasha sat in my office chair
and twirled around in circles, clearly
avoiding my question.

"Don't worry about them. They can't hurt us here."

This little girl was all of a sudden creeping me out and I let out a sigh of relief when Evan came over and took her away.

"Time to go to the library" I said to Jeremy.

"Wanna join me?"

He smiled his beautiful smile and said "Of course. I am really glad you asked."

I got the Scenter book out of my desk drawer and we walked over to the elevator. A hand appeared out of nowhere and stopped me, holding me by my elbow.

"Hi Sophia. So where are you going?" Sam.

Crap. And he couldn't help himself - he was staring at my hand in Jeremy's.

"Are you going to introduce me to...?" I didn't let him finish the sentence.

"Sam, Jeremy, Jeremy, Sam."

Jeremy extended his hand to Sam to shake, but Sam ignored him and looked over at me.

"It's almost five o'clock and it's Friday. I thought you had plans with Cecily and her family. Where are you going?"

Oh no. My lie was going to bite me in the ass!

"Yeah I was just going to the library to drop off this book and I am on my way to meet Cecily." Crap!

I did not want him to see the Scenter book. If he saw me with this book, he would know I was researching him. Worse, he would think I was interested in him and was doing my research to learn more about him. Yeah that would be how he would take it. Nope. Didn't want that to happen. Not one bit.

"I was bored and just keeping Sophia

company on the way to the library. You never know what will jump out and attack." said Jeremy.

He was saving me. Thank Goddess for small favors.

"Looks like you have a book yourself. You headed there?" Jeremy asked Sam. Sam immediately hid the book and stumbled over his own words.

"Uh, yea I mean no. I am not going to the library. This book is part of my personal collection. See you later guys. Sophia, don't keep Cecily waiting. Remember - she would kill you if you broke the plans right?" and he was off.

Jerk. I did get a chance to see the book that he was hiding and only caught the first word of the title. Cliders. Cliders? What was that?

I wish I had seen the rest of the title of the book. I guess I will look it up sometime. Yes, I am nosy and no, I don't care. Whatever he was reading it must be something important and I wanted to know what he was thinking before he surprised me with something. Of course, he was one of the few that hid his thoughts very well and I couldn't read his mind sometimes. Cecily was going to have a ball studying with me!

"Hello, Sophia, earth to Sophia."

Jeremy was waving his hand in front of my face and I seriously didn't even notice. I was so deep in thought that all I could do was picture what I wanted to do when I got home.

So distracting. I wasn't even paying attention to the fact that Jeremy was holding my hand again but miraculously enough, I was breathing. Calm down.

"I'm ok. Just thinking a lot, that's all."
I said.

"Jeremy, let's get to the library and let's
get out of here."

All of a sudden, I was really tired of work.

Our trip to the library was pretty
uneventful except for the stairwell janitor
ogre that hit us with his mop and yelled
obscenities so bad I think I blushed a little.
Disgruntled little bugger. Enter library, drop
off book, walk out. Jeremy turned to me and
said, "I thought you were going to do research
or something?" Crap, did I want to lie to him
too? He already heard me tell Sam that I had
plans with Cecily.

"Um Jeremy, I don't really have plans with
Cecily. I don't like lying to Sam but he keeps
asking me out and I am doing everything in my
power to avoid him but now I've kinda run out
of excuses and am going to have to cave soon."

There. I let it out. Jeremy looked at me
with curiosity on his face.

He finally said, "You don't have to cave.
Just tell him you are seeing someone and you
can't go on a date with him, that's all."

He made it sound so easy.

"Jeremy he KNOWS I am not seeing anyone."
Jeremy laughed at this, said, "Sometimes you
are just not that bright huh?", and pulled me
along.

"Hello. I am holding your hand. I always
hold your hand when we are walking around. Sam
was gaping at our holding hands. What do you
think he is thinking right now? That we are
best buddies?"

He had a point. Sam was probably furious
now, and I did not care.

"I guess you're right" was all I could say.

We went to the elevator and we could not have gotten out of there fast enough.

"Where are we going?" Jeremy asked.

Great. I guess my place.

"We can go to my place. I just want to stop by the bookstore really quickly to find a book for some research I am doing."

We walked over to Hannah's bookstore and as we entered, the little bell rang above the door. That bell ALWAYS scared me! I jumped a little and I think that made Jeremy jump. We giggled and continued walking further into the store.

Hannah walked into the main room from her tarot reading room in the back. She was beautiful. She had long wavy brown hair, shiny and perfect. She had green eyes, the color of glimmering emeralds. Hannah was a banshee. And, she was nice.

She was nice, but don't mess with her. One second of hearing her scream will make you mad. She decided long ago that she didn't want to follow in the direction of her family in exacting revenge and keening (wailing, screaming) people to death, so she came to The Lost Petals and opened up a book store. She does have the ability to accurately (and creepily might I add) read tarot and many people from across all realms and dimensions come to her for insight and advice.

Hannah spoke with an Irish accent and her smile always invited you in.

"Hi Sophia. What a pleasure to see you again. And this is?" she asked.

Not only did she ask, but she asked with a smirk on her face. I totally knew what that meant by the way.

"Hannah, Jeremy, Jeremy Hannah. Jeremy is

one of my newer recruits." They shook hands and immediately Hannah stepped back.

"Sophia, can I talk to you for a moment in private please?" she asked. She looked nervous. I glanced at Jeremy and guessed he took the hint because he walked away and browsed the shelves.

"What's up Hannah?" I asked her.

"Did you know that he has suffered great loss? He is one big vision of hurt."

"Yes I know. He lost his parents to a car accident and foster care wasn't that great. But how did you know that?"

I already knew the answer as I asked the stupid question. She could catch on peoples past and their past lives. It started out with the tarot and she just built it up over the years.

"Sophia, be careful with him. He could get attached too soon and it could end badly for the both of you."

Just what I was afraid of - but really, who was getting attached faster - him or me?

"Thanks Hannah. I appreciate your concern. I will be alright, don't worry."

I walked away before she had a chance to say something else.

Jeremy was off to the side looking at some crystals Hannah had for sale. His eyes glowed with fascination at the different types of crystals and medallions available. The dim lighting overhead and bright lighting on the tables made the shadows dance on the walls. I walked over to Jeremy and he put his hand on my hand.

"Wait" he said.

"Wait here for me and don't move."

Before I could say anything, he hurried off

into the other room to speak with Hannah. They were in there for what seemed like days but they finally came out and Hannah was laughing at something he had said. Jeremy walked over to me, smiled and grabbed my hand.

"So Sophia what were you going to look for here?" Jeremy asked. I was so caught up in all of these other little intricacies I almost forgot why I wanted to come here.

"Hannah, do you have any books about Cliders?" I asked.

Hannah just gave me a solemn look and motioned me over to a small cabinet. She removed a key from her pocket and unlocked the cabinet to reveal several very old looking books. The smell was musty to a tee!

"I have only one book about Cliders and it is in here. It surprises me you are looking for information on Cliders as they are not very common on our plane. Do you need some help researching? Is it for a recruit lead? I can try to contact some of my colleagues to see if they have anything else that might be useful if you would like."

Hannah was still looking at me and I swear she thought I had officially gone mad. Should I tell her I didn't even know what a Clider was? Should I tell her that the only reason I wanted to look up Cliders was because of stupid Sam? Ugh! I did what I normally do in situations such as these - I lied.

"Well a new recruit overheard some folks at F.L.E.S.H. talking about them and asked me what they were. I don't really know what they are so decided to come to you for help. I just knew you would have something to reference."

She kept staring at me with shining green eyes and the overall aura of calm and relaxation. I was actually getting sleepy. She was reading me. Reading my reflexes. Reading my breathing. Reading my nervousness.

"Well Sophia I will loan you this book but be very careful of what you learn. Much of the information in this book is very disturbing."

She was starting to scare me and she knew it.

"I'll be sure to keep that in mind. Thank you Hannah. I will take care of the book and return it as soon as I am done. C'mon Jeremy. We have to go do that thing."

He was leaning over a table covered in feathers - Raven, ostrich, clawfoot, grintan - all feathers that have been enchanted or cursed, whichever way you want to look at it. I tried to stay away from that kind of stuff. Jeremy picked up a raven feather and asked "how much for this?" Hannah smiled and told him he could keep that feather, it was on the house.

"Hopefully it will prove to you the majick here is true and you will come again to make some purchases."

She pulled out a bag and put the feather in it for him. He thanked her and took my hand. As we walked out of the store, Hannah whispered into my mind "remember what I said about the book. Be very careful."

As we walked hand in hand back to my apartment, I told Jeremy that he should perhaps go back to his place. I was tired and needed to get some sleep. I had another assignment tomorrow and needed to regain my energy (and I needed to eat and I didn't want him to be with me to see that because I was embarrassed).

He surprisingly agreed, but said he would

walk back to his place only after he walked me home to make sure I made it safely. He was so cute. I mean, I was the Flesh Craver here. I was the one who would be able to protect both of us if anything tried to harm us. Too cute.

We passed a few Pleasers and quickly walked past - their moans and screams blending in with the night air. Yuck. They are one of the many things I am actually afraid of. Weird because it's like guaranteed food but there's something about someone forcing it on you. Not my style.

We got to my apartment building. Jeremy leaned into me and whispered in my ear "have a good night. I will be thinking of you", gave me a quick peck on the cheek and was off. He hurried along and disappeared into the night.

I finally made it into my apartment and sat on the floor in front of the couch. I needed to start reading this Cliders book now. The warnings from Hannah and the hesitation in Sam's voice when Jeremy asked him what book he had got me thinking way too much. I had to read!

CLIDERS

Chapter One: History Lesson

The word Clider comes from ancient Entymian times stemming from the word Cli meaning Soul and Der meaning thief.

Blah blah blah. That's all I wanted to know from chapter one.

Chapter Six: What do Cliders do?

Cliders roam the dimensions in search of souls. They capture the two extremes: pure souls and evil souls. The only way they can exist is to feed their bodies with the souls of others. Cliders can take on many shapes, sizes and forms. They can clone themselves into whatever form their victims are to be accepted into their world. When the victim is comfortable and trusts the Clider that is when the Clider will strike and snatch the soul. The soul is removed by a strand of Clider hair that is like a needle. The hair needle is inserted into the victims neck and the soul is sucked out into the strand. Once they collect the soul they eat the strand of hair and the soul enters their bodies. They will gain all memories, intelligence, etc. from the souls they collect. Once the soul starts to wither, usually within one month, they must collect another soul. If they cannot find a soul to collect their physical forms will die and they will cease to be.

CHAPTER ELEVEN: What happens to the bodies of the beings whose souls are stolen?

The physical body withers and dissipates within seconds. Those who are unfortunate enough to have their souls stolen will live within the confines of the Cliders mind. In there the soul is subject to unspeakable torture and pain. It is taken to another world of rage, anger and hatred. If the soul is a pure one the torment is unbearable. If the soul is evil it will live its last moments in pure ecstasy, enjoying the torment and pain.

Okay, enough reading for me. I still don't understand what a Clider really is but at least I had something to start with. I wonder why Sam was reading up on Cliders? They sound horrible! I don't think I would want to associate myself with a Clider so why would Sam?

DEAR DIARY,

Friday night was interesting. I don't know what's gotten into Sam but he's been acting weirder than normal. He seems to be sneaking around a lot and it feels like every time I am with Jeremy at F.L.E.S.H. he pops out of the shadows and asks us fifty questions. I know he is in love with me but wow he needs to get the hint.

Jeremy on the other hand has also been acting a little shady. He continues to go to his lessons on becoming a Flesh Craver and has been asking me lots of questions. That I don't mind. However, he has also been dodging me a lot. The other day we were out to lunch and he looked at his watch, got up and kissed me on the cheek and said he was going to be late and he was sorry and he would make it up to me. Didn't say why or where he was going. I tried to bring it up but he kept changing the subject. I let it go, but it's really starting to bother me. Cecily was right - I let him in too soon and now I am way past obsessive.

I had a good time on Saturday night with Melody. We watched a cheesy B movie only we could enjoy about a little girl who had a doll that came to life and went on a killing spree. Hey, it could happen, right? My throat kinda hurts because of all of the steam I had to conjure up in my apartment but it was well worth it just to see Melody smile.

I went on another recruit lead case (which by the way was another one of Evans' not so great assignments). I was attacked by a

Vandion. Explanation: A Vandion is a shape shifter - can shift from human form to some sort of giant scorpion thingy. Of course F.L.E.S.H. was interested in this thing because of the damage it could inflict on others. Just one sting and the prey is dead on contact. Not all beings are affected by their sting, but most are. The Vandion rushed me in human form, grabbed my arm and twisted it behind me and held me close to him. He asked me what I wanted, I told him it was his choice, and he chose to send me packing with a fractured elbow and a nice gash on my neck thanks to his sharp nails, claws, whatever.

As I entered and exited Reflection World, I passed Max but this time he wasn't with his Angel wife. DIARY! I am so happy! I am finally starting to get over him!! I hope that's what it means anyway. He waved at me and I smiled but for the first time in YEARS I didn't feel claustrophobic within myself and the vast emptiness around me. I was okay. Cecily will be so proud of me! Good night, sweet dreams, tomorrow is another day.

8 HUNGER HURTS

So, at work the next day, Henderson came around my cubicle and sat down in front of me.

"So, howsabout you and me, tonight, romantic duo collection? We can take on another couple or we can take on the same person. The rush alone will be amazing."

Yuck and gag me! I hate him.

"Henderson please leave me alone. You are so disgusting. Maybe you should rethink your approach. Just don't practice on me anymore."

He smiled, let out a sigh, shrugged and said "your loss" and walked away whistling.

My desk was starting to look like a paper recycling plant and I needed to organize quickly before Evan told me to do so. I sorted through all of my case files and placed them in importance from high to low. As I opened up my file cabinet, Jeremy poked his head in and cleared his throat. Yes he scared me. Yes I jumped.

"Oh jeezus you scared the CRAP out of me! You really need to stop doing that. One of these days I am going to have something sharp in my hands and take a swing" I said, hoping to not sound too upset.

He looked down at my hands (oh and his hair was doing that cute thing again where it fell over his eyes a little bit and he had to reach up and pull it back behind his ear) and smiled.

"Well I guess I lucked out this time. You didn't have a sharp object."

Having said that, he sat down and stared at me.

"What?" I asked.

He was being shifty again and I did not like it one bit.

"Nothing" he said, excessively fast.

"I just like watching you at work."

I chose to ignore him and kept organizing my desk. After about ten minutes, he got up and stretched.

"Hey so I was wondering if you would like to come over to my place tonight. I can say for dinner, but I won't have anything you would eat. But we can watch a movie?"

I looked down a little embarrassed and said, "sure, what movie do you have in mind?"

"Don't know. Maybe we can just wing it. I have lots of movies at home we can pick from. So pick you up at 8?"

I told him I would meet him there and he had no choice but to agree. He left but not before kissing the back of my hand. What was UP with him?

The little red light on my phone kept telling me I have been ignoring voicemails for over a week now. Blech. I had so much on my mind. Cliders, Scenters, weird creepy girls with creepy cloaked figures in her Reflection World, and Jeremy. Now was not the time for checking voicemails. As I was finishing up organizing my desk, I came across a small piece of scrap paper folded twice. It had been set partially under my telephone. I picked it up, opened it and it read:

STOP INVESTIGATING. IF YOU DO NOT STOP, YOU WILL BE STOPPED.

I dropped the paper onto the floor, it looked up at me, and I swear it laughed. All of a sudden, it was gone. It disappeared into thin air. Did I imagine it? Am I getting paranoid? I checked under my desk, under my chair, under my bookshelf and it was definitely not there. I think I needed to eat.

I hadn't eaten in a few days and one of the things they teach you in our Essentials and Fundamentals of Flesh Collection is that you can't let too much time go by without collecting. Weird things start happening to you both mentally and physically. Hallucinations was one of those things. I must have imagined that piece of paper. Not even sure what it would mean anyway.

Deciding to go to Cecily's for a makeover was useless - Cecily wasn't home. Her mom and dad had not seen her all day and she hadn't called. This of course was not a shock to any of us because sometimes Cecily would disappear for days at a time with no explanations and then come home saying she was stuck under a rock because it was too sunny where she was and she didn't want to risk getting out and dying.

I didn't buy any of her excuses - the truth HAD to be better right? I think the next time I talked to her, I was going to sit her down and force her to tell me exactly who she had been sneaking around with. She says she isn't doing that but I so don't believe her.

Her mom lets me come and go as I please into Cecily's bedroom so I walked in there and she had left me a little note on her nightstand. The outside of the note said "read me" - had to be for me right?

Sophia, don't come looking for me. I will be back home as soon as I am done with this thing I need to do. Don't worry, I will be fine and I will be back in a flash. Love, Cec. P.S. How's Jeremy?

Hmmm. That's odd. Her notes are not usually this.......nice? Whatever. She's so sneaky. I guess I'm on my own for my makeover.

Ever since my experience last time with Reflectioning, I have been hesitant to do so. I have been dreaming of those red beady eyes, and would at times wake up in cold sweats. I couldn't let that get the best of me

As fast as Reflectioning is, sometimes it feels like you are in there forever. All packed up and ready to go, I unearthed my mirror and headed into Reflection World. As I crossed through, the scene was unlike any other I have experienced on my own.

The atmosphere was stuffy and I was having a hard time breathing. The colors around me were browns and oranges with a touch of black here and there. Off in the distance I could see figures coming toward me and they seemed to be getting closer, faster.

Typically, I can pass through and find my way to the other side. This time however, I focused on the different scenes and the figures so much I lost my light. I became frantic, twisting and turning around looking for my escape loop.

The figures were moving faster and I could see the cloaks now. There were three of them and they were coming right at me. I was on my hands and knees searching for the escape and I felt tears well up in my eyes, the lump in my throat growing larger with every passing second. I was so disoriented I didn't even know where I had come from.

The cloaks were close enough for me to see that they were brown, dark brown and they were covered in red (blood?). I closed my eyes at this thought and kept feeling my way, hoping to find something to hold on to, something that would lead me either back to my office or to my collection. My hands found something soft on the ground.

I opened my eyes and to my horror it was a body, well, what used to be a body. It was twisted as if someone had wrung it out like a hand towel. Bones were sticking out of it in multiple places. For a moment, I forgot all about the figures and looked at this body with amazement. Part of me wanted to take a couple of chunks and dig in. Hey, I'm not squeamish. After all, I AM a Flesh Craver, right? On the other hand, this body smelled a little off.

Before I could have another thought, I saw shadows in front of me covering the body's face. The cloaked figures were behind me. Immediately I smelled the stench of sewage and death. Too petrified to turn around, I slowly started crawling away. Once I was around the body, I stood up and made a run for it. Still searching for my light, I looked back and saw the figures were right behind me.

As I ran, I glanced over to another scene and this time I saw Max but he looked all weird. His face was pale and his eyes were bloodshot. He was hunched over and looked like he was in pain. One of his wings had a large tear on the end. I ran over to him to see what was wrong (yes I KNOW this is not real but it felt real!).

When I reached him, he cringed from me and fell onto the ground. He looked up at me and I saw blood pouring from his mouth. I asked him what happened and he just pointed behind me. As I turned around, I saw one of the cloaked figures feasting on Max's perfect Angel wife.

The creature was tearing her apart! Max's eyes were pleading for me to help. I didn't know what to do, so I ran. When I started running, the creature noticed me and of course ran after me. The others were just behind it. I barely made it back to my apartment as the creature grabbed onto my leg.

Back in my apartment, I winced. The damned thing scratched me and it actually took. Usually when something happens to you in Reflection World, it doesn't come back with you (except the trauma in your head). This time the scratch came back with me. AND it actually hurt.

I bandaged the stupid scratch and before I knew it, I was running out of time for my date with Jeremy. A quick shower, whatever for the clothing and absolutely no time for makeup, I WALKED my way over to Jeremy's place. Walked being the key word. My trip there was pretty uneventful, except for the throbbing that was beginning to ooze its way out of the scratch on my leg.

When I got to Jeremy's apartment door, I was feeling a bit faintish and my vision was getting blurry. As Jeremy opened the door, I collapsed into his arms.

"I'm hungry" was all I said as he caught me. The last thing I remember was looking up at Jeremy and biting a chunk out of his arm

9 EXPLANATIONS PART 2

I woke up in a puddle of glomulis. I felt it, smelled it. Disoriented, I opened my eyes. Jeremy and Hannah were hovering over me with concern and fear in their eyes.

"Sophia! Are you ok?" asked Jeremy.

He ran over to me and got down on his knees. I was lying on the floor with a pillow under my head. Munchkin had made a bed on the floor behind my knees. She got up, came around to my face, smelled me and walked away.

"I feel like throwing.."

As soon as I said that, my stomach made gurgling sounds and I spewed whatever else may have been left in my stomach. Unfortunately, Jeremy was so close to me it somewhat projectiled all over him. The embarrassment was enormous.

I closed my eyes to avoid having to make eye contact with him. He on the other hand grabbed a towel he had nearby, wiped his face and hands as best he could, and continued to hover over me with concern.

"Shhh," Jeremy said.

"It's ok. Get it all out. Hannah says it's poison from those cloaked things."

I tried to ask some questions but every time I opened my mouth, I felt like I would spew again so I decided to just lay still and be quiet, hoping the feeling would soon pass.

"Sophia, you were very lucky to get out of there alive," said Hannah.

"I came over here as fast as I could when Jeremy called me."

I glanced over at Jeremy and he was holding an ice pack on his head. Oh no! He had a vision of me in Reflection World. That's how he knew!

Guilt immediately set in for Jeremy having to go through the pain of a vision of me.

"I'm so sorry Jeremy" I whispered.

And, I threw up again.

"Stop talking Sophia" said Jeremy.

"Get some rest."

I closed my eyes and fell asleep.

As I slept, I heard Jeremy and Hannah talking. I heard words like "she's very lucky" and "don't know what we would have done if you hadn't had that vision" and "I think the poison is almost completely gone".

I also heard Jeremy thanking Hannah over and over again for saving my life. Going in and out of consciousness was challenging.

One moment I was eavesdropping on their conversation, the next I was dreaming of the cloaked figures hovering over me, drooling on me, tearing me apart. I had the horrible images of Max's Angel wife in pieces and the cloaked figures eating her flesh, tearing her wings and shredding them; Max's face in pain and helpless, unable to save her.

Wake up Sophia! Wake up! I did not want to keep reliving this nightmare! I awoke with a startle and once awake I felt the pain. The pain that only meant one thing: need to feed.

"I need to eat," I whispered.

Jeremy just chuckled.

"My arm not enough for you?" he mumbled.

Was he being serious or sarcastic? I kinda

couldn't tell.

"Just kidding, I can't say I have ever had anyone actually bite off a chunk of my body but that really hurt! I would do it all over again if it meant I would still have you here with me," he said.

Under other circumstances, I would have thought that pretty romantic but at this particular moment, I wanted to hide under a rock for 200 years.

"Jeremy, I'm so sorry. I don't know what came over me to do that to you when I saw you. I was so hungry and traumatized and didn't quite have control of my hunger. I let it go too long. Are you ok?"

He looked down at me and smiled.

"I'm fine. I guess that I can consider it one of my lessons in flesh collection. Remember to recite your spell or your potential will feel excruciating pain. Yep. They don't lie."

I stumbled out of the bed.

"I will be right back. I am going to quick collect and then you can tell me what in the hell happened to me. What are those figures? What did they do to me?"

He looked at me as if I had six heads.

"You are not going ANYWHERE," he said.

"Obviously those things are targeting you in Reflection World and you are going to have to deal with me bringing you food until we find out what they are and what they want."

At once, I felt at ease. I really did not want to go back into Reflection World. I was truly afraid.

"I made some calls to the office and a volunteer feeder is in the living room ready to donate to you. I will wait in here if you want."

He was so cute and sweet.

Mazzy was the volunteer. Twenty five years old, loved working for our corporation and very happy to help.

"Hi Sophia, I'm so happy I can help you. It is always an honor and privilege to offer my flesh to natural born Flesh Cravers."

I recited my spell (although volunteers don't need false memories implanted into their psyche. They remember how they were injured. The spell is mainly for no pain).

After I collected a chunk of her thigh (which is by far the yummiest part of the body in my opinion), I helped get her bandaged up and sent her on her way. I noticed a piece of my leg had started to rot. It was discolored - blues, greens and yellows all combining into one oozing gaping wound. Once I ate, that spot immediately healed up along with the area where the cloaked figure had grabbed me and apparently poisoned me. I felt refreshed and alive (undead?). Whatever. I felt good.

Jeremy walked into the living room looking like he had been hit by a truck.

"I think an explanation is order," I said.

He took my hand and sat me down next to him on the couch. Munchkin took her rightful place on his shoulder.

"Okay. Here is what happened. As soon as you stepped foot into Reflection World, I had this vision of you being attacked by those cloaked things. My vision of course made me convulse and pass out for a few seconds but I dragged myself to the phone and called Hannah. After explaining what they looked like she said she knew what to do and came rushing over here."

"When you got here, she was already inside ready to heal you AND me because I also knew you were going to bite me. While you were puking your brains out she explained these cloaked figures are out for flesh IN Reflection World."

"Call them the evil zombies of Reflection World. They are nasty creatures who once they get their sights set on what they want they will stop at nothing to get it. By grabbing your leg, the cloaked creature poisoned you with some sort of tracking venom. This venom would not have killed you but would have made you WANT to go back to Reflection World and offer yourself to them. They would have invaded your dreams, charmed you so to speak. They are called Drünods."

"Hannah had a potion she injected into you to drive the venom out but you had to upchuck it. Hannah said no one really knows much about the Drünods, only some smaller texts elders were able to extract from the caves. They managed to get just enough information to come up with a cure for Flesh Cravers by extracting the venom, but there is no cure for other beings as of yet. This potion has killed every other being the elders have had to try to cure. If it had gotten me, I would be dead by now."

As Jeremy spoke, he kept pulling his stubborn hair over his ears and while I was hearing him, I wasn't REALLY paying attention. I wanted to kiss him. He kept clutching his head and checking on his arm where I bit him. I was so selfish. He saved my life and I just wanted to kiss him.

"Jeremy, I can't thank you enough for saving me. To think I would have voluntarily gone to those disgusting creatures is horrible. I'm so sorry I bit you. What can I do to make it up to you?" I asked.

"Well" he said. "I think you need to get some rest for the evening so date night is out. And you um, kind of smell badly from all of the nastiness that's caked all over you" he said.

Oh, dear, Hiliad! I was still covered in my glomulis. Uber grossness.

"Uhh, I think that's a good idea Jeremy. I can't believe I am sitting here talking to you covered in this stuff. I'm going home."

He reached over and touched my face.

"Sophia, I want nothing more than to hold you and spend the rest of the evening with you but Hannah gave me specific instructions. Let you get home and sleep. BUT, I am walking you home - no Reflectioning for a little while. There are the volunteers at work that can feed you until we figure out how you will be protected from these things."

How could I argue?

He walked me home. We said our goodbyes, I hopped in my shower and finally was able to clean the grossness off me and actually smell halfway decent. I fell into bed. Sleep would NOT come easily. Images in my head, questions I had to ask, what was going on? I picked up my phone and called Cecily. Right to voicemail. Where WAS she???!!

I supposed I should actually get some sleep since that's what the doctor ordered. But, every time I closed my eyes I couldn't get the image of the Drünods out. Poor Max. I hope that image wasn't true. I actually fell asleep thinking of Max. Thinking of the times we had together. Thinking of the past and what could have been. Wait. Jeremy!

10 JEAOUSY CONQUERS ALL

So, the next day Jeremy came over to check in on me. I was still a bit queasy from the day before and I'm sure I looked like hell.

"How are you feeling today?" he asked.

"Like a million bucks" I teased.

He knew I didn't feel well but I guessed it was one of those things you just had to ask.

"Evan said you could take the day off if you still weren't feeling up to par so I told him I would deliver the message to you," he said.

"No Jeremy. I want to go back to work. I have a recruit lead I just can't ignore. It is another little kid. The longer I wait the longer this child is in danger in their world."

He laughed a laugh of cuteness.

"Sophia! You absolutely amaze me. If you think I am going to let you into Reflection World you have another thing coming."

I can't believe I hadn't even thought of going into Reflection World. Stupid.

"Oh. Yeah. I forgot about that," I said.

Jeremy sat down on the couch and held his hand out to me. It's amazing at how much I wanted him to hold me.

"Come sit with me. Let's relax a bit. After all, you've had a rough couple of days."

I took his hand and sat with him. He put his arm around my shoulders and held me close to him.

He mumbled "you have no idea how much I was worried about you. When I had that vision of you, I thought they were going to kill you and I could do nothing about it. This time I did it. I was able to control the future and change the outcome. Sophia, if I hadn't fought through the pain of my vision and contacted Hannah, you would have belonged to those cloaked things. I never would have forgiven myself."

He caressed my face and brought me closer to his.

"Can you just stick with me until we figure out what's going on please?" he asked.

How could I say no?

"Jeremy, why are you going to all this trouble for me? It seems like I'm just dragging you into my web of badness."

He leaned into me and smiled.

"You, my dear, are worth going through all the badness in the world if it means we can be together."

And we kissed.

This kiss was different.

It was softer, more passionate.

It was not filled with the sadness and desire to feel. It was filled with care and lust.

Oh yeah, we were both in way too deep.

He traced a line down my arm that drew all of my goose bumps out from hiding. I caressed his arm where I had bit him and quickly moved my hand away, not wanting to hurt him. As we moved closer into each other, our breathing got heavier.

My heart was skipping beats. We fell into each other's embrace, letting ourselves fall into this abyss of a kiss.

Jeremy moved his mouth over my chin and down my neck. As he gently pulled my hair away from my neck to continue, a brilliant light lit up the room. Oh no! What bad timing! The light was blinding and Jeremy grabbed onto me for dear life. He pushed me behind him and grabbed the first weapon he saw – my lamp. Goddess, he was adorable!

"Jeremy, it's ok. I know who this is. Put the lamp down," I said.

"What?" he asked.

"Why do things want to keep attacking you?"

"It's not an attack," I said.

Jeremy put the lamp down and waited. The light dimmed and all that was left was Max.

"Sophia, long time no see. I see you are busy right now. Is it a bad time?"

I sighed. "Max, what are you doing here?" I asked.

"You're the Angel from Reflection World" Jeremy said.

I guess some introductions were in order.

"Max have a seat. Jeremy have a seat."

I did not even know where to start. Max began the conversation for me.

"Last night you were thinking of me, I sensed it. I felt it. So, I came today to see how you were doing. Obviously, you are doing him. I mean fine."

Was Max exuding jealousy? "Max this is Jeremy, my.."

Before I could finish my sentence, Jeremy cut me off.

"Boyfriend. Nice to meet you, Max is it?" Jeremy said. Jeremy was being a little sarcastic and pulled me close to him.

"Oh, I see," said Max.

"From what I sensed last night it seemed like you were missing me Sophia. Was I wrong?" Max said, almost a little too cocky for my liking. Oh, what a jerk. I could not believe Angels could be so, so, possessive. I also could not believe I was calling an Angel a jerk. I hope whatever higher power was out there didn't hold that against me, if it even applied to me at all!

"Sophia, is this the guy from Reflection World? Who the heck is he?" asked Jeremy.

"I am her EX-boyfriend," replied Max. Emphasizing EX.

"Okay, EX-boyfriend. What do you want?" asked Jeremy.

There was so much snarkiness in Jeremy's voice it was sickening. Max looked at Jeremy and I swear there was hatred.

"Like I said, Sophia was thinking of me and it must have been some good thinking since I sensed it. So, I came to her rescue. Sophia, what WERE you thinking about that brought me here?" asked Max.

Oh boy. Now they were BOTH looking at me.

"Alright, alright. Enough testosterone here. I was thinking of you MAX because I saw you in Reflection World being attacked by some cloaked creatures and I was hoping you were OK. Now that I KNOW you are ok you can go now."

He flinched.

"You want me to go?" he asked.

"I came all this way and you want me to go?"

He crossed his arms and sat firm on the couch, his beautiful Angelic wings tucked away, neatly bending with the curves of his wonderful body.

"I'm not going anywhere until you tell me more about this attack in Reflection World. And, if I'm not mistaken, aren't you supposed to see your innermost desires in Reflection World? So you saw me? How does your BOYFRIEND feel about this?"

Jeremy just smiled but I felt him inch a little closer to me.

"Well Max. Sorry to burst your bubble but you ARE mistaken. Reflection World isn't just about your innermost desires. It's about reflections of your past, future, present as well. Clearly Sophia has been seeing you in Reflection World because you were a part of her past."

I think he chuckled. Max didn't seem amused.

"Max, can you just go now please?" I asked.

"Thank you for coming all this way to make sure I was ok and I am glad to see you are doing well too but you have to go now."

Max looked up at me and we made eye contact. Bad move. His Angel eyes captured my gaze and I was drawn in.

Immediately, all of my feelings for him came rushing back into my heart and I had visions of us together, of when we were happy. He kept staring into my eyes and smiled his Angelic smile. I was always a sucker for his smile. Max's eyes glowed like the sun.

As I continued to gaze into those majickal eyes, I noticed I was swaying back and forth, much like a pendulum hanging from a string. Back and forth. Relaxing. Relaxed. Comforting. Comfort. Loving. Loved. Peaceful. Peace. Sway. Back. Forth. Looking into those eyes, I could feel peace; I could hear bliss. I could smell love and passion. I could taste Heaven.

At once, Jeremy got in between us and broke the gaze.

"Is he working some sort of majick on you Sophia? Max, buddy, it's been great, but you heard her. Please go."

Max looked at me once again and said "are you sure you want me to go? I can stay, you know, catch up, talk about the good old days and such?"

His voice was like a million string instruments playing in my head, ringing in my ears. Playing to the beat of my undead heart. Playing to the tune of my sway.

"Yes. I'm sure." I mumbled, but I almost said no. His eyes had consumed me. The question was, did I really want him to leave?

Max got up, spread his wings and his bright light lit up the room again. One of his wings knocked into Jeremy's head sending him tumbling over the couch. I think Max smiled as he faded off into his stupid bright light.

Once Max was gone, I ran over to the other side of the couch to help Jeremy up.

"Jeremy, are you okay?" I asked. He had a wing burn on his temple.

"Yeah, I'm okay. Sophia, you dated an Angel?! Why didn't you tell me this before tonight so that I could have been a little better prepared for this surprise visit?" He asked.

"Jeremy, don't get all jealous on me. The subject of exes hasn't exactly come up in conversation between us just yet. I don't know who you have dated right?"

Okay. I know it wasn't fair.

"I dated humans. Humans. Not friggin Angels. I think your dating history is a little more important than mine right now," he said.

He was right. "Sorry Jer. I wasn't trying to hide it."

Wasn't I?

We went back around the couch and sat down. I quick ran into the kitchen and got him an icepack for his temple.

"Thanks" was all he was able to mumble. Was he seriously upset with me?

"Sophia, what Max was saying about Reflection World and innermost desires, was he right? Do you see him in Reflection World because you still love him? Is this why it's been so hard for you to let me into your heart?"

Seriously? He was flooding me with all of these questions right now? When just ten minutes ago we were on this very couch getting really intimate and he was asking me these questions NOW?!

"Jeremy, Reflection World is a combination of feelings and emotions. You were explaining it to Max just fine. Why are you questioning me about it all now? I can't really explain it in massive detail right now since you are kind of jumping down my throat for no good reason. I was thinking about Max because my experience in Reflection World was disturbing and we dated for a very long time so you can't expect me to not feel ANYTHING for him. So let's drop it for now please?"

He heard the frustration in my voice and his entire demeanor changed.

"I'm sorry Sophia. I don't know what got into me. I guess I saw the way he captured you with his gaze and I wanted to be the only one who could have that effect on you."

Now I felt bad.

"Jeremy, look. You are the one in my heart right now. Yeah, I still have those feelings locked away for Max but that was in my past as you said. We are here now, together, and think of this. Max is an Angel. He has that Angelic gift to be able to have that effect on me. You are still human and you have managed to capture me with your gaze from day one. How's that for a thought?"

He thought this through for a few seconds and seemed to relax a little.

"You're right Sophia. I'm sorry for acting like a jealous freak. It's just that when you come to the realization that you are competing with an Angel, you kind of think you have already lost as a human. I mean, what can I offer you that he can't?"

After careful consideration and trying to find the right words, I said "You. You can offer me You."

I leaned in and kissed his forehead. I pulled the stubborn hair from his face to behind his ear and whispered in his ear "It's you I want Jeremy."

It was at that precise moment that I knew I meant it with all of my heart.

EMOTIONS ARE EVIL

After Max's surprise visit, Jeremy stuck around for a while but left in a hurry. I still didn't know what he was doing being all sneaky and such but once again didn't have the nerve to come right out and ask him. Once he was gone, I called upon Max. It took a matter of 2.5 seconds before he showed up. Bright light. Beautiful, silky white wings. Max.

"Max, before you even start with me I want to make one thing clear. What you did back there was totally uncalled for."

He had a smug look on his face and sat down, his wings neatly folded with his body. Oh, his body. Stop Sophia! Focus!

"Sophia, I apologize if I made you uncomfortable. I came because you called for me. You thought of me enough to send for me and that's the only reason I came. If I knew you were sucking face with some random guy on the couch, I certainly wouldn't have come to see you."

Typical male.

"Kissing. We were kissing. And anyway, who are you to judge what I am doing? Just because I am in a relationship now doesn't give you the right to be.. the right to be…"

And I couldn't find the words I wanted. Why? Because our eyes met again.

"Sophia, I'll tell you what. Let's not fight. Let's be happy. Are you happy with this Jeremy guy? Even though he is a human and you are going to outlive him and he will die within a blink of an eye in your time frame? If he makes you happy, then that's all that matters. I was actually very happy you were thinking of me and called out to me because I have missed you so much. You're not only seeing me in Reflection World because you are thinking of me, but because I too am thinking of you. I've been wanting to do this for a long time now."

He leaned in and kissed me. Not just any kiss. An Angel kiss. For anyone who has not been fortunate enough to be kissed by an Angel, let me explain. Any moment of happiness turns to bliss. You are locked in that kiss and the world stops. You can almost get lost in it; it puts you into some sort of trance. And once I realized what Max was trying to do, I pushed him away.

"Max stop it right now. I can't believe you. All of these years have passed, we have seen each other maybe a dozen times and no word from you otherwise. We see each other now, and now that I am dating someone finally, now that I am happy, you pull this crap on me? Not happening, Angel or not. Now that I know you are okay you can go now. I just wanted to talk but I guess you can't handle talking."

He looked at me with those eyes and I had to look away.

"Stop it Max. You are not going to mesmerize me again. That's cheating and besides, do you really want to win someone with your majickal eyes?"

He looked down. Finally, he was thinking clearly.

"Sophia, when I saw you kissing Jeremy it just took me back to us. I was jealous. I am jealous. Just because I'm an Angel doesn't mean I don't have feelings. At that moment, I wanted to hurt him; to send him away from you so that I could hold you. I know I should fight those feelings and bring out nothing but peace and happiness in every situation but I too was once human and the feelings kind of came back with a vengeance. I was jealous. Is that so wrong?"

Now he sounded cute and wanted my sympathy. Jerk!

"Max look. Of course I miss you and of course I have been thinking of you non-stop. But, believe it or not, I have finally moved on. You said it yourself. WE can't work; not with your responsibilities as an Angel. It just won't work. And besides, aren't you married?"

When I asked him that question, he took a few steps back.

"No I'm not married. Do you think I would be here if I were married? Where did you get such a silly idea?"

Now I felt like the jerk.

"Oh, just me believing the stupid things I saw in Reflection World."

Stupid, stupid, stupid. I just can't help always making myself look like a child.

"Sophia, what you see in Reflection World could be anything. You could have just called for me and asked."

What was he doing? I don't need any more explanations.

"Well Max, now that we have cleared many things up, it was great seeing you. Take care of yourself ok?" Max walked over to me, looked down at me and caressed my face. I avoided eye contact and looked down.

"Sophia, I'm glad you have moved on. The reality is I have never stopped loving you. My responsibilities as an Angel forced me to leave you. If it were not for that, we would still be together. Many times I have thought of turning in my wings to be with you. Please don't ever forget that."

He kissed me on my forehead, put his head down, stretched out his wings and vanished with his blinding light, all with his hand caressing my cheek.

Stunned, I sat down on the couch. I reached up and touched the tingling on my forehead. It was warm. It was electric. How I had missed that feeling. How I had missed Max and his calmness. How I had missed his kiss. Calm down Sophia. This was good. This was closure.

What I was feeling now were the remnants of Angel mojo. They don't mean to do it all the time, but when they want to make you feel special, loved, desired – they sure get the job done. Being sidetracked by his Angelness won't get me anywhere right now! Time to go back to work and at least review my case files.

Breathing exercises on my walk to work helped a lot. My emotions were going crazy, but I had held it together with Max. I wondered what Jeremy was up to. Was he thinking of me? Had I betrayed him by hashing up old feelings with Max? Now I wanted to get to Jeremy more than ever.

Sometimes I hated how I always overcomplicated things. Max was Max. He was my love for so many years. When he left me, I was heartbroken. Seeing him again did make me happy, but what made me happier was the fact that I was able to see him and not fall all over him like I had envisioned I would do if I ever saw him again.

This was good. Jeremy was really in my heart. I couldn't stop thinking of him.

Pleasers Run was eerily full. They were lingering in the shadows and hundreds of arms were flailing out, waiting to catch the Flesh Craver that came within two inches of their alley. They are not allowed to leave the alley you see. They will instantly be taken back to their plane of existence. But if a Flesh Craver gets close, they can pull them in and force feed. I always walked across the street, didn't want to risk it. My luck I would trip and fall right into their alley of rancid death.

Running up the steps to F.L.E.S.H. was special. I tripped over my own two feet because I had jinxed myself when I was thinking of Pleasers Run only to have Sam catch me before I took a nose dive back down the over two hundred steps. "Hi Sophia." He muttered.

I gathered myself and looked at him. He looked different. His face appeared to be clearing up and his hair looked less greasy than usual.

"Hi Sam. Thanks for the catch." I said. He smiled.

"Sophia, I wanted to tell you that I am working really hard to prove myself to you. I want you to see it in everything I do. Can you just give me that chance?"

Here we go again.

"Sam, I don't know what to say that's not going to hurt your feelings. I just don't see you that way. You have to understand. We can't continue like this, day in and day out. You are a friend to me, kinda of like a brother. An overprotective, annoying brother at that. Don't make this more complicated than it is."

He looked genuinely sad.

"Sophia, I will never give up trying. Please try to make it back to your cubicle without hurting yourself" and he was off.

Why does he put himself in these situations?

Back at my cubicle Evan had put about fifty more case files on my desk. I swear does anyone ELSE work here for crying out loud? Now that my super important case file was buried under these new ones, it was time to organize in order of importance. Let's see what these case files were all about.

There were several case files that would require me to go into the Shadow Realm. Several more yet that would require me to go to the planet Tharion. Tharion is very far from earth but is really similar. Humans and all. Well, I guess the word "Human" can be interpreted a little differently in the case of Tharion.

Tharion humans are all mute. They don't talk to each other. They think to each other. They don't have mouths. It's really cool and creepy at the same time. I don't want to go there just yet. Tharionians are not a very peaceful bunch, again, much like humans. Since they have psychic powers, they like to think they are above everyone and everything. The truth is, only one in every one million are ever recruited by us because they are traitors by nature. I don't want to go there at all, so this case file is going to the bottom of my pile.

More case files for places I really didn't want to go to. When I sort by importance, I look for children. Evan might sort differently for me but I can't stand the thought of children out there, alone, afraid, wondering what was going to happen to them because of their "unique" ability. I would rather help them first. So sue me.

The next case file I came across was one of Mintara. This one touched a place somewhere in my heart and I had to keep reading.

Case file of Mintara Levhiri

Full Name: Mintara Levhiri (Nickname Minty)
Address: Cave 104 degrees, Northern Ice Plains, Freeze Dimension
Phone Number: n/a
DOB: Born early 1300's however age slowly. Approximate age 18 human years.
Height: 5'0 Weight: 120lbs
Occupation: Employed by Ayce Corporation as an Ice Thrower instructor.
Medical History: Unknown
Medications: Unknown
Family History: Parents both work for Ayce Corporation. 3 siblings; Garaf (older brother, 19 human years), Nizra (middle brother, 17 human years), and Jempi (youngest brother, 16 human years). Mintara is the only daughter and the youngest of all siblings.
Mental Health: Killed a cousin while developing her powers in ice throwing. Not very happy her parents have forced her to work for Acye Corporation as an instructor.
Lead Information: Minty has been monitored for 2 months. Her work takes up approximately 2/3 of her day and her nightlife consists of family time. Appears to be a

close family and brothers keep an eye on her. Minty appears sad most of the time and does not appear to have many, if any, friends.

Daily Itinerary:. Wake up at 5am. Walk to work by 6am. Work from 6:30am-3pm. Home by 4pm. Start making dinner for the family.

Pets: One Orwi (dog-like creature able to survive in the Freeze Dimension) – named Kookers, age approximately 1 human year.

As I reviewed this case file, my mind kept wandering back to Max. All these years missing him, actually convincing myself he was happily married with a beautiful Angel wife and all along, he was missing me too. Confusion was starting to rear its ugly little head into my mind, and before it was able to go on any longer, Jeremy popped into my office. It was so good to see him!

He sat down and looked up at me. His stubborn hair was calling my hand to push it back behind his ear but Jeremy's body language appeared to tell me not to.

"Sophia, I have been thinking about our future together and I think we should spend some time tonight and talk about how we feel for each other. Call me sappy, whatever. I don't want to freak you out but ever since meeting Max I am feeling really inadequate for you. Maybe it's jealousy, maybe it's lack of self-esteem, but I want you to know how much I can offer you if given a real chance."

I sat there not knowing what to say. He continued.

"I had a vision, you see. This one was of you and Max, very happy together. In my vision

Max killed me. He killed me and he looked down at me and smiled. I never thought I would be unhappy to see my life end. All this time I have spent mourning the death of my parents, cursing my so-called gift and now, now I have you. Only for me to die? At the hand of an Angel? I don't think I'm ready for that just yet."

I was appalled and didn't know what to say. Max would NEVER kill Jeremy. It was just impossible. We really needed to talk because I think Jeremy was starting to create these visions all on his own out of jealousy.

"Jeremy, clearly we need to talk about us. I don't want you to think for one minute that Max is going to kill you and that I am going to let him kill you and be happy about it! Let me make you dinner tonight at my place. We can finally spend some time together and sort things out."

He looked down and sighed.

"Ok Sophia that sounds like a plan. I will meet you there around 7."

He got up and left. No goodbye. No twinkle in his eye. Nothing. Great. Now I felt like a complete jerk, thinking about Max and Jeremy was insecure. Maybe this is why I haven't dated anyone since Max. The drama. I had to focus on work because if not I was going to go absolutely insane.

Minty. How could I get to Minty but not go through Reflection World? As I was pondering that thought, Sam popped into my cubicle and threw himself on a chair, one leg dangling over the arm. Honestly, doesn't anyone work around here?

"Sophia, what's up? What's your latest weirdo recruit lead like?"

He had a smirk on his face that worried me because he was usually all broody.

"What's up with you Sam? You are all happy and chipper."

He smiled at me and turned his head to the side. I could see in the light now just how much his face had cleared up and his hair actually looked shiny and soft, not greasy at all.

"Oh nothing" he said.

"Just wanted to stop in and see what was up is all."

Ok now he was beginning to creep me out again.

"Sam. I really need to work on my recruit lead here but I can't go into Reflection World just yet. I'm afraid."

I don't know what possessed me to be so honest with him. I mean, at that moment, I didn't really think anything of it. But looking back, I should have known his reaction.

"I'll go with you. I'll protect you. Sophia, let me do this for you."

And here we were on this roller coaster ride of romantic denial.

"Sam, I don't think this is a good idea. I mean don't get me wrong. Thank you for offering.." and he cut me off.

"Sophia, I'm not taking no for an answer. Let's go."

Fast as lightning, he raced over to me and grabbed my hand. He whispered the spell and we were off into Reflection World. We whizzed past Max who was sitting on a rock with his head in his hands, sobbing. We passed black cloaked zombie figures that turned their heads my way, opened their crooked mouths, pointed and let out one of the worst screeches I had ever heard. Then they started running towards us. Sam held onto my hand so hard I thought he would break something but before I could think anymore, we were on the other side in the Freeze Dimension.

"Where to next my pretty little lady?" he asked with a smile on his face, and yes, he was still holding my hand.

Maybe he was taking advantage of the situation but I was alright with that. I had felt safe in Reflection World. I never thought Sam, out of all people, could provide that for me.

"I don't know exactly where to go. Minty should be here somewhere."

"Minty? Her name is Minty?" he asked. He doubled over and started laughing.

"What kind of name is Minty?"

I let go of his hand because hello, he was acting like a jerk.

"Her name is Mintara and Minty is her nickname. Stop laughing and acting like a child and help me look for her. Reflection World wouldn't just dump us here if she weren't around."

I swear he had tears in his eyes from laughing so hard. After a few moments to gather his composure, he steadied his breathing and smiled.

"Sorry, that just struck me as funny, that's all."

"Just help me find her." I snapped. I was getting annoyed. Thank Goddess Hiliad he was annoying me. This seemed normal. Good.

As we walked on this path in the Northern Ice Plains, I couldn't help notice the beauty of this dimension. Everything was white. Ice trees, ice benches, ice everywhere. Icicles hung from ice trees in decorative designs creating colorful swirls at every glance. The grass was covered with frost and was waving back and forth with the slight cool breeze. Iced daisies and daffodils swung with the breeze and I could smell the sweet aroma of the flowers with every step we took.

Sam walked over to some of the flowers and picked a few up. He handed them over to me with a shy smile on his face.

"For you. I've always wanted to do that."

As soon as I touched the flowers though, they wilted and fell to the ground, then disappeared.

"Aww…why did that happen?" I said.

"Oh yeah. Everything in the Northern Ice Plains will die if touched by anyone or anything other than the cohabitants of the Freeze Dimension. We can't touch it for more than a few seconds and poof they are gone. It's so that we can't take them back to our realms and figure out the chemical make-up of this planes' unique freeze properties."

He kept walking and I wondered how he knew so much about this.

"How do you know all of this?" I asked.

"Oh, I like to read." He said.

"Sometimes I will just go to the library and settle in to a really good book. One day I just happened to pick up a book on the Freeze Dimension, but it only gives you the basics. We really don't know too much about the Cold Ones which is probably why you were sent here to pick up Minty."

And he smiled at her name.

"Stop laughing!" I snapped. But, I couldn't resist a small chuckle myself.

From the corner of my eye, I noticed something moving from behind a tree. I saw a young girl which could only be Minty. She was beautiful. Her complexion was extremely pale, unlike any other being I have ever seen.

Her hair looked like fresh icicles but pliable and soft. It looked like waves in a frozen ocean if you could picture that. She had ice blue eyes and lips of deep purple. She had all natural makeup which made me kind of jealous. She was a sight to see. I glanced over at Sam and he was looking down, clearly not impressed.

"Mintara?" I asked. "Are you Mintara?"

She slowly walked our way and said "you don't belong here." She kept walking towards us with confidence I only wish I could possess.

"What are you doing here?" she asked.

"We are here to offer you a chance to join us." I said.

She smiled and ran over to me. Sam immediately stepped in front of me and put his arm out.

"Stay back ice demon!" he yelled.

I pushed him away just as Mintara let out a frightened shield of ice. It bounced off of the ground and shattered onto a nearby tree.

"Stop it!" I yelled.

"Everyone just chill out!" And at this, Minty let out a laugh.

"Nice choice of words."

Sam looked over at me and smiled. He was proud of himself for trying to protect me and I thought he was brave for doing it. Maybe he isn't so bad after all. Stop Sophia! Focus. Minty. Jeremy. Minty.

Mintara walked up to me and took my hand.

She was so cold her touch gave me goose bumps.
"What is your name?" she asked.
"Sophia" I said.
She led me over to a bench and sat down. I sat with her and immediately stood back up.
"Ouch! This bench is so cold!" I muttered.
She laughed.
"Of course it is silly. It's made of ice."
Sam stood next to me, arms crossed over his chest looking like a nightclub security guard. He circled around and stood behind her. I glanced over at him and saw he was watching her like a hawk. What I noticed most of all was that he was sniffing her. His nostrils were going crazy. I wondered what he smelled.

He scrunched his nose over and over again and his eyes turned this incredible pale grey color. He found something. I have never seen him do this before. What did it mean? His eyes got paler and paler grey and he inched closer to her, all the while his nose was working overtime.

I think he was sensing my glares as Mintara jabbered on because he quickly looked over my way and his eyes went back to normal. He looked down, almost embarrassed that I had seen him. He stepped back and walked over to a tree. Hmm. What was that all about?

"Sophia, ever since I was a little girl, we were told these bedtime stories. Stories of recruiters coming for special people, but I never imagined in a million years you would come for me. I am so excited!" she gasped.

"Wait, can I say goodbye to my family and friends?" she asked.

Since this was not the human realm, it was alright for Minty to go to her family and friends and say goodbye. They knew we existed.

They have heard of us and our recruiting. Some beings actually wanted this to happen to their children. They saw it as a sign of respect and great achievement to be a chosen one. I didn't get it.

"Yes you can go say goodbye to your friends and family. Let's meet back here in half hour." I told her.

She smiled and quickly ran off. I think she skipped a little bit.

"Alright Sam. Spill it. What did she smell like?" I asked.

He came around the bench and sat down.

"I'm sorry you had to see me like that Sophia. I had promised myself to not show you that side of me."

I looked over at him and he had his head down.

"Sam. You are a Scenter. This is what you do. Why do you seem ashamed of it? Why are you always hiding from me?"

He looked up at me and said, "I am ashamed Sophia. It makes me feel not normal. I can't simply be a Flesh Craver like you. I hate that I am not an original like you are. A true born Craver. I had to be made. I had to be chosen because of some stupid scenting gene in my bloodline. I have never really accepted scenting as being a part of who I am because I feel like it makes me an animal. I don't like to be considered an animal."

Oh Goddess was he going to cry? I hate crying.

"Sam, you ARE normal. Don't you see? Ever since you were recruited and turned, you have been such a huge help to the corporation. Your scenting abilities have led to so many captures of traitors and evil within the company. You have to see how important you are."

He just kept looking up at me and let me rant on. I don't know what possessed me to say so many nice things to him. Maybe I felt sorry for him? Maybe I was starting to actually like the guy (you know, in the non- romantic sense)? After I was done with my rant, he continued to sit there and look up at me. It seemed like forever but he finally spoke.

"If I am so great and normal, why can't you love me like I love you?"

Sigh. Back to square one.

I didn't know what to say, as usual. At that moment, Minty popped in and saved me from having to answer.

"Can we go now?" she asked, clearly very excited to be leaving her realm.

"Yes, we can go now. I will give you all of the details once we get back to the corporation."

I stood to Sam's left and Minty stood to his right. He held our hands and took us through Reflection World so fast, I didn't have the opportunity to see anything, no Max, no Drünods, no car accident, no Mallies. Just zipped back into my office cubicle.

He wished Minty a pleasant transition and was out. He didn't even say goodbye or give me the chance to thank him for helping me on this case.

"Boy is he cranky or what?" Minty said.

"He'll be okay" I said.

"He just needs time to adjust to some things that are not quite going his way."

An orienter took her away, and if I didn't get going, I would be late for my dinner with Jeremy.

12 DINNER?

By the time I got home, I only had a half hour to get ready. I had stopped at the human food deli and picked up some steak and potatoes. I bought some rosemary and butter for the potatoes and some salt and pepper for the steak. Nothing fancy.

Just preparing the meal grossed me out so much I had to race into the bathroom to throw up. I could not wait for Jeremy to transition into Flesh Craver so that I would not have to deal with this nasty sad excuse for food. I had felt some grumbling in my stomach and should really have eaten something at work but of course, I was running late and didn't think of it until now.

I had just gotten out of the shower and dressed when Jeremy arrived. He was dressed in jeans and a black t-shirt. His hair was falling all over his face and he looked sad. I invited him in and hugged him.

"I have missed you so much Jeremy," I said. "Dinner is in the oven, almost done. I hope you like steak and potatoes."

He smiled at me and quickly looked away. "Can we talk before we eat?" he asked.

I really wasn't ready for this conversation, but agreed. He looked like he needed to vent and well, I guess I had no choice but to listen and console.

"Sophia. My vision was so vivid. So real. Max killed me with some sort of sword; it was a golden sword with an emblem on it and some writing. I couldn't catch all of what it said but sometimes I can't immediately remember the things I see in my visions and remember them later. I'm sure it will come to me in a dream and when I wake up I can quick sketch it, maybe we can find out what the sword is and where it comes from. Anyway, while I was dying I saw you walk over to Max and the two of you were standing there, looking down at me and laughing. You were laughing."

He continued.

"When I came to after my vision, I felt horrible. My entire life my visions have been one hundred percent accurate and it wasn't until recently in my life that I promised myself if some of my visions were not right, were bad, I would try as hard as I could to do something about it and change the outcome. I was so proud of myself when I changed the ending of my vision of you with the Drünods in Reflection World. I'm just nervous now because I have absolutely no idea how I could change this vision."

I started to speak, shaking my head and he put his finger on my lips.

"Don't talk yet. Let me finish please."

I sat back and let him do just that.

"You see, since I met Max and found out about him being an Angel, that's all I could think of so I started doing some Angel research. I need some information from you. What kind of Angel is he?" he asked.

I mumbled "Serminian".

"Are you positive?" he asked again.

"Yes" I said, and he sat back.

"Okay. The Serminian Angels are actually good. They shouldn't have evil thoughts or desires. I'm trying to figure out why he is going to kill me."

"He's not going to kill you Jeremy!" I snapped. "You're telling me stuff I already know. I think that you are jealous and the encounter the other day really made you feel uncomfortable and I am so sorry that you had to go through that. Nevertheless, you have to understand that Max and I had a very long history together and he was trying to make sure I was alright. Please believe me when I say that he and I are over and that I really want this to work with me and you."

He looked at me with his head partially down and stood up.

"Well yeah that made me really uncomfortable. Especially the way he was looking at you. I mean he is an Angel. Isn't he supposed to respect you and me? Isn't he supposed to wish nothing but good thoughts and blessings for us to be happy? I didn't see that in his look and I sure as hell didn't feel that in the atmosphere. And, as much research as I have done I really feel like he is going to kill me due to human emotions. Jealousy. I will fight as much as I can for you Sophia and know I will but I just don't think I am a match for an Angel."

He got up and walked over to the kitchen.

"I think the food is done."

He smiled at me and for a split second, I saw Jeremy coming back.

"You really don't have to sit and eat with me Sophia. I know how sick it makes you. I am getting along in my studies and wow I can't believe you have sat with me to eat this food knowing how grossed out you are." I chuckled.

We went from this serious conversation to dinner and food talk and I was just going to let it go. I really wanted to just enjoy a night with no drama. No distractions. Just Jeremy and me.

"I will sit with you while you eat. I just want to spend time with you. We haven't exactly had a nice relaxing time together." I said. I served him his dinner and internalized the grossness that was rising up to my throat. I tried my hardest to not let it show and I think he noticed because he ate his food so fast it was gone in like ten minutes. "All done!" he said.

"And thank you for cooking. It was excellent."

He stood up and cleared the table. When he came back, he took my hand and kissed the back of it.

"I really don't want to be the jealous freaky boyfriend. I want to make you happy. I want us to be happy. I'm confused right now but please give me time to understand what is happening here."

"I am suddenly in this different world, transitioning to be a Flesh Craver. I have met Scenters, demons, Angels, fairies, gnomes, ogres, you name it. These beings just 6 months ago I thought only existed in fairy tales. I dream of this beautiful girl for months and suddenly she appears, in my apartment, and asks me to join her in her world. It was the moment I had been waiting for my entire life. Let me try to make you happy and prove to you that I am the one for you."

He was so sad. He was so happy.

I decided I would make the next move. I led him to the couch and touched his face (and of course I pulled his hair back behind his ear, I absolutely LOVED doing that!). I had each one of my hands on either side of his face, leaned into him, and kissed him. Just a soft almost non-existent kiss. He put his arms around my waist and leaned in closer. We kissed and caressed each other and it was the most fantastic feeling.

We paused for a brief moment and he sat back.

"Alright. I have a feeling this is going to get…"

And I didn't let him finish. I pulled him to me and kissed him with all that I had. I felt him smile under my lips and I smiled back, never stopping the kiss.

In the blink of an eye, I felt the rush of feeding. The rush of collecting. I felt my eyes, the all too familiar ecstatic feeling of pure feeding pleasure, roll back into my head and saw white. I felt my blood pulse throughout my entire body and my instincts kicked in. I searched for the perfect collection spot on Jeremy. It was his arm. I bit him. Hard. I took a piece off and he jerked back with astonishment.

"Sophia, what's happening?!" he gasped.

He held his arm and grabbed a throw from the couch to stop the bleeding. I could see him as if I was under water. The waves of hunger and the moment of feeding bliss was still inside of me. He had interrupted, and I wasn't done.

I didn't know what was happening to me. This was the second time this happened with Jeremy and if I didn't stop it I was going to kill him. I have never not been able to control my hunger. What was going on?!

With gooey bloody chunks of his arm in my mouth, my hunger was growing stronger. I chewed on the tough flesh and the drool was starting to collect and drip from my mouth. In a very sad attempt to control this hunger, this craving, I thrust myself onto my ceiling and cringed away into a corner. My necklace was increasing in heat, pulsating with my rapid heartbeat. It felt as if it would leave burn marks on my flesh.

I looked down at Jeremy, the waves still circling in front of my eyes and distorting everything in the room. I began to cry.

"Jeremy I need you to leave. I need you to get Hannah. Or Sam. Someone who is not human. Please do it now! I don't know what's going on. Hurry!"

I held on tight to one of the rafters on my ceiling.

"Sophia, I am not leaving you alone! I will wait until you calm down a little bit."

I felt my hunger begin to take control of me and I crawled closer to him, my arms reaching out to him to cut, tear, break away any flesh I could come in contact with.

"LEAVE!" I screamed.

"Okay. I'll leave. But you can't be left alone." And he did something I never thought he would do. He called for Max.

"Max. Max, Serminian Angel. I call to you. Please come quickly. I need your help."

He was walking around the apartment and with his every move, I crawled closer and closer to him. I realized my hunger was getting so bad that I was drooling long, globs of nasty drool. Deep down inside I was so embarrassed.

"Max where are you?!" Jeremy yelled.

"Sophia's in trouble and you need to come now!" As he yelled the word now, he slammed his hand onto the dining room table.

I guess that was enough for Max to show up in his heavenly light. He took one look at Jeremy and said, "What is going on here?"

Jeremy took him out into the hall and I don't know what they spoke about. I crawled quickly to the door, still on the ceiling with my head dangling now, trying to hear but I couldn't. The hunger had completely consumed me and I was helpless. I needed to feed and I needed to feed now. Max walked in alone.

"Sophia, Sophia, Sophia. What are we going to do with you?" he said.

He smirked and whispered something. In an instant, I was dragged down from the ceiling and wrapped in some Angel chains. They didn't hurt. They were just binding. He sat me down on a chair and I was now chained to it as well. He whispered something again, and the chair had bolts and now it was bolted onto the floor. I wasn't going anywhere.

Max sat in a chair across from me and smiled.

"Sophia, I'm going to help you get through this. I'm here for you."

He came up to me and kissed me on my forehead. His kiss left an electric shock of warm fuzzy goodness. I didn't feel the need to feed on him because he wasn't human. This was good. Every minute that passed, I felt my hunger passing and my eyes finally rolled back.

I don't know how long I sat there, grunting, squirming and craving flesh, but after a while I felt like myself again. Max was holding my hands the entire time. He had been looking into my eyes, sending heavenly calmness into my body. His every touch tingled and warmed me.

"Are you feeling better now?" he asked. I mumbled, "I'm hungry" and passed out.

When I woke up, I was alone. Max was gone and I was no longer chained to his Angelic chair thing. I walked around my apartment trying to sort things out in my head. What happened? Why was I alone? Where was Max? Where was Jeremy? I hope I didn't hurt them.

Well I know I couldn't possibly hurt Max but what was most important was Jeremy. I picked up the phone and dialed Jeremy's phone number but there was no answer. I called out to Max to come to me and after a few minutes of trying, he never showed up. I felt full. I felt satisfied. What was going on? I tried to call Hannah and again, no answer. Where was everyone?

I felt alone, abandoned. What had happened to me? Why did the hunger consume me and make me all crazy? Why had I lost control of it? I've never had this happen to me and I needed answers. I tried one last phone call and finally got an answer.

"Meet me at the library at F.L.E.S.H." I said. "Hurry."

13 SURPRISES

When I walked into the library, I saw Sam sitting at one of the tables. A literary Fairy greeted me at the door and I pushed my way through, getting annoyed with their chipper natures. Must be nice to always be so happy. Sam noticed me walk in, got up, and pulled out a chair for me. I sat down and put my head in my hands.

"Sophia, what's wrong?" he asked.

"You scared me a bit and I almost Reflectioned to your apartment."

He looked concerned. He looked scared. He looked worried. Under the fluorescent lights, I could see his face was completely cleared of all blemishes and actually looked smooth. His hair was fluffy and he had gotten a haircut, short and spiky. He looked different. He also looked more confident. I don't know, he was being weird.

"Sam, something happened to me today and I don't know what's going on."

I explained to him the chain of events and he listened. He watched me and the few times I glanced over at him, I noticed he was staring at my mouth. When I got to the part about Max chaining me up in the Angelic chair, Sam's eyes grew increasingly greyer. Was he getting angry? What was he feeling?

"Sam, snap out of it," I said. "What are you thinking?"

"So here's the deal Sophia. I think someone is messing with you. Who have you ticked off? What have you done to make someone hate you so much to want you to suffer so much?"

I think I almost fell out of my chair. I don't do anything to anyone. I mean, I try not to anyway.

"Sam, I don't even know where to begin to think here. You seriously think someone is out to get me? Why? Why would someone want to do these things to me? I don't think I've made anyone angry. I mean, I don't really have much of a life. I work, go home, work again. Hang out with Cecily. That's it. I don't have time to piss people off."

Sam was watching me again. This time, he got the creep factor going for him again. His nostrils were flaring and his eyes darkened by the second. First dark grey, then lighter, then lighter until his eyes looked like a wisp of a gray cloud in a blue sky.

I watched as the hairs on his arms stood up and his posture changed. He whipped his head behind him and let out a growl.

Now, I've never seen Sam's true Scenter side. Scenters don't actually turn into wolves, just certain characteristics change. Like now, he was intuitive, sniffing, scenting. He caught something in the air. The hair on the back of his neck started to grow just a little bit, another Scenter trait, and his growl grew louder. Instantly, a literary Fairy came over and kindly asked us to leave.

I touched Sam's hand and he whipped his head back to me. I broke his concentration. He stood up, grabbed my hand and dragged me out of the library. He didn't speak to me. I was trying to ask questions, but he kept dragging me through the halls of F.L.E.S.H. We went into the elevator, onto another floor passing darkened hallways.

Where were we going? What was he doing? He put his hand over my mouth to keep me from talking and after a few minutes, I showed him I would keep quiet. We must have been going at it for about fifteen minutes, in and out of rooms, stopping for just enough time to catch my breath, and he would drag me again to our next destination.

Another hall, another corner, a restroom, a classroom. He finally guided us into an auditorium and found a mirror. He Reflectioned us so quickly I didn't have time to be afraid of the Drünods.

When we entered Reflection World, it was different. It was all Sam. There I was, looking at me. Lots of me. Me with him at a diner. Me with him on a couch watching a movie. Me with him dancing. Can we say stalker? I didn't know what to be more afraid of, Sam or the Drünods. Sam's grip on my wrist did not let up. Where was he taking me?

We exited Reflection World and we were in a house. The room we Reflectioned into was neatly decorated with dark greens and blacks. Brilliant green crystals hung from the ceiling creating reflections of perfectly shaped diamonds on the walls that gleamed with the light bulbs. The room was simple. Bed. Nightstand. Desk.

Sam walked over to a painting on the wall and looked up at it. A small light scanned his eyes and the wall shifted, opening up into another room behind this one. A secret room - really? I followed him into this room and it was surreal; books everywhere.

There were two tables in the center of the room and there were two stories of bookshelves lining every square inch of the walls. Sam closed the door/wall behind us and told me to sit down.

He did not give me a chance to speak again. He crouched down to the ground, sniffed up in the air and leaped up to the second story landing in front of one bookcase. This bookcase was special. It looked like it held valuable books, old books.

There were glass panes that looked almost bulletproof. He moved his hand over the side of the bookcase and it opened up for him. He skimmed through the books and pulled one out. He jumped down to my level and sat next to me. He placed the book on the table. I didn't even have to look at the title as I already knew what the book was. Cliders.

"Sam. Tell me.."

He shushed me. He walked around the room mumbling something under his breath. A small glowing light traced the entire room from floor to ceiling, around all of the shelves and flowed around us. I felt the warm tingling sensation of majick.

"For protection" he said.

"Now, we talk."

"See Sophia, I've been watching you. Not all creepy like you think I am, I've been protecting you. All these books here help me help you. When we bump into each other, it's not an accident. Whenever I come near you, touch you, I sense things. I can sense when something bad is going to happen to you. I can smell it. I can almost taste it. When you first introduced me to Jeremy, I wanted to find something about him that was wrong. I wanted him to be evil. I didn't want you to be in love with him."

"All of my research and I still can't find anything about him. I am not only a Scenter, but I am what you call a Clairsentient. I have this psychic ability to sense when something significant is about to happen. But, that's not good enough. I can't do this alone. No majick in the world can get me what I need to help you. So, books it is. And a little help from some friends."

"Being a Scenter I've met a lot of beings in my life. Being a craver I've met an equal amount of special beings, some I even call my friends. I have recruited some beings I trust to help me figure out who is behind all of this, and I've lost all of my contacts. You need to tell me what has happened recently to make you vulnerable to these attacks. When did they first start?"

As I thought back through the past several weeks, I really couldn't put my finger on what was happening. My life hasn't changed all that much. I haven't been mean or vindictive to anyone. Ugh! This was so frustrating!

"Sam, do you know where Jeremy, Hannah and Max are?" I asked.

"When I went through the hunger takeover, Jeremy and Max were there, then it was just Max, and then I was alone. I tried to call them all and I haven't been able to reach anyone. You were the only one who answered."

He smiled. Not a creepy smile. A warm smile. A smile that almost said, "it's because I'm the only one you can count on."

I hated it when he was placed in these situations, but glad he was here to help. I felt safe with him.

"Sophia, I don't know where they are. All

I know is, I got a call from you just after I had returned from a scenting job, you were frantic, and I was there. I am really glad you called me."

And he smiled again.

"Keep thinking while I go get you some food."

He stood up from his chair and I swear he was getting taller. Oh I wished I had actually paid attention in class when we were reviewing majick and Scenters and Cliders. Stupid stupid Sophia! Why was he changing so much? What was he up to? Where was Jeremy? And Max? And Hannah?

As I tried to think of more clues to these strange and dangerous events, I kept going back to that weird little note I had found in my office, the one that poof, disappeared.

I had thought it was a hallucination, but could it have been real? Some of this crap started when I met Jeremy. Was it Jeremy? I couldn't bear the thought of Jeremy wanting to hurt me. And where the hell was Cecily? I needed her more than ever!

Sam came back with some snacks for us. They looked very fresh and I wasn't complaining. While I munched on some "finger" food, he pulled out a book I had never seen before and started to explain some things to me.

"Sophia, you don't know much about me. You haven't taken the time to get to know me. That's ok. I understand I am not your type. I'm not Jeremy. And I'm certainly no Serminian Angel. But just hear me out. I haven't stopped progressing as a Scenter. I know you haven't paid attention to your studies because you keep looking at me like I'm a different person. I'm still changing. I'm still growing."

Sam said this with pride.

"I'm still developing my powers, my instincts. Being turned into a Flesh Craver didn't change that part of me. I'd have to say I am more Scenter than Flesh Craver at this point. I can go for weeks without feeding because I can control it. My decomposition slows down. My healing increases. My adrenaline takes over and I can focus on what is important - my prey. Being a Scenter, Flesh Craver and Clairsentient, I have an edge on a lot of other beings."

At that moment, he kept talking, and I stopped listening. My hunger pangs came back with a vengeance. I flipped the table over, the lantern flew across the room, and I barely got to see Sam sprint with his ultra-fast speed and catch the lantern before the room caught on fire before my eyes rolled back into their sockets and I, once again, went hunger crazy. And once again, my necklace seemed to be burning right through to my soul.

Sam raced over to me and held me in his arms. I didn't feel the need to feed off him. He grabbed some of the food he had brought in and fed it to me, one piece at a time, patiently. All the while, he had me in a bear hug.

My vision came back into focus and I could see him now. He was taller, stronger. Crap he must have grown 6 or 7 inches. How had I not noticed that? He was still holding on to me while I sucked down the flesh, drooling and snapping the entire time. My glasses had somehow made their way up to the second floor of this library room and I couldn't see very well, so some things were a bit blurry. But not Sam. He was very close, and very clear.

He caught my gaze. Light grey. Dissipating clouds on a rainy day. A hint of yellow sunshine beyond the clouds. Calming. Soothing. Relaxing. My hunger rage was going away. Sam did it. He helped me. He carried me over to an old rust colored Victorian lounge chair and put a pillow under my head.

"Sleep, Sophia. Sleep. I will help you figure this out."

I was exhausted. I was full. I slept, and I dreamt of Sam and his grey Scenter eyes. Wonderful. Just wonderful.

14 THE LOST ARE SOMETIMES FOUND

When I woke up, guess who was there to greet me - all cheery and smiling? Yep! Sam. He brought me some blood to drink in a coffee mug (mixed with some flesh of course - its consistency is much like a chunky smoothie). He had clearly been up all night, researching, investigating. He looked tired, but alert all at the same time.

"Good morning gloomy sunshine! How did you sleep?" he asked.

He sat next to me on the now very uncomfortable lounge and stared at me. I looked away.

Whatever majick Scenters had with their eyes (what was it about eyes these days?), I wanted nothing to do with it.

"I'm feeling ok I think" I said.

My head was a little fuzzy and my back and neck ached a little from this old lounge, but other than that, I felt fine. My mug of chunky goodness made me feel better as I drank.

I looked around the room and noticed Sam had put everything back in its place. The table was in order, the lantern was once again lit and creating beautiful silhouettes around the room, dancing silhouettes. The fireplace was glowing and the room was warm and comfortable. My glasses were neatly folded on the table next to me. I looked over at Sam who was just sitting next to me, looking at me. He almost seemed to be looking through me.

Creepy! This was good. Again, I was a little creeped out by him. I liked that. Creepy was good. None of this adoration crap. I couldn't possibly handle that right now.

He must have noticed a change in me (damn his intuition!) because he got up and paced for a little while. He glanced my way and seemed lost in thought. I slithered out from under the blanket and walked into the bathroom.

I noticed Sam had set out some spare clothes for me to change into. Clothes. Ugh! Did he go into my apartment and go through my things? A knock on the door made me lose my train of thought and I jumped.

"Yeah?" I gasped.

"I thought you might want to freshen up and get a shower. I put a fresh towel out for you and got you some clothes."

He said this all innocent-like. I was still in shock with the clothing he chose for me. Ways in the depths of my closet were my "dress" clothes. Long, flowery skirt that draped down in layers to my ankles, flowy top that hung loosely in every which way.

He brought my underwear and bra. Matching set. Embarrassed, I crept into the shower and washed up. I did notice before creeping into the shower that Sam had removed the mirror from the cabinet above the sink. Thoughtful, or did he not want me to escape?

When I was done, I stepped out of the bathroom feeling like a new woman. I was clean, I was full and I wanted answers. Sam sidestepped me in my determination to his giant collection of books. Anything! Everything! I wanted to know what was happening.

"Sam, did you find anything out while I was asleep?" I asked. He shrugged.

"No, not really. I did get in touch with Hannah and she said Jeremy is okay. She contacted Evan and asked that he be monitored and watched. Whatever is coming after you may want to target him so we can't be too careful."

I thought for a moment. Why didn't Jeremy try to reach me?

"Sam, can I borrow your phone please? I want to call Jeremy."

He looked at me and his mouth opened. Then he shut it. His eyes started to turn that silvery gray. He hated when I said Jeremy's name.

"No can do sweetie," he said.

"Can't make any calls from here. Can't let anyone know where you are. It's safer that way."

"Are you holding me captive?" I asked.

Hey, it was a valid question. He didn't let me make any calls. He went and got my clothes (again, creepy), and he wasn't giving me much information. Sam walked around the table and sat down.

"I'm not holding you captive Sophia. I am trying to protect you. You are more than welcome to go if you'd like, but you would be making this so much harder than it has to be. Why can't you just sit still, let us all help you in trying to figure this out, and then you can go be with your precious Jeremy who you have only known for a short amount of time."

"I mean, you don't know ANYTHING about this guy. For all you know, HE could be the one who's trying to hurt you. Me, on the other hand, you have known for over 40 years. You were my recruiter. I have been in love with you since the first day I met you and have done nothing but try to prove myself to you. There have been no others for me. Yet you seem to trust Jeremy more than you trust me. I just don't get it."

He walked away and turned his back to me. Before I could say another word, he leaped up to the balcony and immersed himself in a giant book of what I could only assume to be more research. Why couldn't he just use the stairs? Did he always have to make such a production out of everything?

How could he make this about relationships? He was so blinded by his jealousy that he couldn't see what this was all about. Well Sophia, what WAS this all about? If I couldn't explain it, how could I expect Sam to understand it? Well crap. I guess I should start reading too. I noticed a book on the table (among a gazillion books on the table, but this one in particular stood out in the crowd).

DAEITIMENIES

Chapter 1: Dr. Trimon and Gundar

Daeitimenies are vengeful yet peaceful creatures. Earlier captive Daeitimenies have provided modern science with some varying information on their capabilities and their objectives as a species. In the late 1400's, a young scientist by the name of Frederick Trimon studied a Daeitimeny named Gundar. Dr. Trimon was only 18 years of age, a young natural born Flesh Craver, who devoted his life to researching and studying foreign species.

Dr. Trimon stumbled across Gundar after finding him injured during an inter-species war. Gundar had severe head wounds and internal bleeding. After many months of treatment and recovery, Gundar had come to trust Dr. Trimon and decided he was no longer a prisoner. He would work with Dr. Trimon to help him understand his species. In return, Gundar only asked for safety, food and shelter.

Gundar was approximately 180 years old. He had learned to speak English through their earthly studies courses as a child and spoke very well. He trusted Dr. Trimon with many Daeitimeny secrets and told countless stories of his travels to other realms. Dr. Trimon learned that Daeitimenies are very much like humans. They look just like a human. Their differences were immense.

While they had essentially the same diet, Daeitimenies were natural vegetarians. They feasted only on plant-life and seed. Gundar explained that while they were similar to humans, they are more of an evolved species; evolved in their modern medicines and healing. They have cured all diseases and ailments that have affected Daeitimenies and once shared their secrets with humankind. However, they quickly learned that humans were not to be trusted. Humans used the cures within their government research facilities, murdered and hunted any and all Daeitimenies within the realm of Earth as to not release to the public that there were indeed cures to cancers and other deadly diseases that are the common killers of humans. Their explanations were these cures could shut down politics and pharmaceutical companies for good, leaving politicians, government agencies and the likes of them to live normal lives without all of the frivolous monetary gains they were currently obtaining through these "ridiculous human laws", as Gundar would put it.

Dr. Trimon listened and took notes. He watched Gundar as he would injure himself and with herbs would heal these wounds within minutes. Once, Dr. Trimon asked for the cure for cancer and Gundar refused. He said he would take these larger trade secrets to his grave. Dr. Trimon watched Gundar grow and eventually die.

Gundar lost his life due to old age, something, he said, they could not avoid. He welcomed death much like a child welcomes a bottle. He learned to love Dr. Trimon as a son loves his father. Dr. Trimon mourned. He had only spent 10 years with Gundar and he too, had learned to love him. The following are excerpts from Dr. Trimon's daily journal entries.

Ugh. I can't keep reading this. What the hell does any of this crap have to do with me? I mean, something out there clearly wants me to either die or kill someone and I want to go do something about it, not read stupid books that are going to make me fall asleep.

I mean seriously. Why? My frustration must have oozed all over the room and I knew Sam noticed. He jumped down from the balcony (again, can't he use the stairs?) and stood in front of me.

"Listen Sophia, for as long as you are here, can you please make the best of it? I do not want to fight. I do not want to argue. I am trying to make this comfortable for you. This is your escape. No one will find you here. Can't you just accept that? Do you have to release your misery through your pores?"

He sat down and looked pouty. Sheesh. I didn't think I was being that bad.

"Sam, I'm not miserable. I just really want to know what is happening. Can't you use some sort of majick to find out? I mean, c'mon. You and I both know I am not the greatest with majick, but you are awesome at it. You're pretty much awesome in everything you do!"

Okay, okay. I was trying to get to his ego. Maybe, just maybe, it would work. He smiled. He looked over at me and truly smiled. With that smile, he grinned.

Through the grin, he muttered, "we can't use majick in here or they can find us. I did one majick spell of protection and that is it. I have to leave now, can't raise suspicion if both of us are gone right?"

He started to walk away.

Within an instant, he turned around, looked me in the eyes and muttered "oh, and if I'm so awesome at pretty much everything I do, why can't you love me?" and he walked away.

Ouch. Again, jealous little freak. It's hard for me to even like him right now. If he is trying to help me so much, why is he being such a big baby? He did his little retinal scan thingy to open the bookshelf door and he was out before I could argue.

I took the opportunity to scan the books. As I searched through rows and rows of books, I couldn't help but wonder how he had set this all up for himself. I mean, this was a really cool set up. Cherry wood bookshelves lined both levels from floor to ceiling. The shadow play from the lantern and the fireplace provided movement all over the room. The warmth of the room made me feel homey, at peace.

Scanning through the books, I came across titles such as How to not howl at the Moon and other short stories for Scenters. I had to laugh at this one. Master of your Gift. Common Craver Mistakes. All books I probably should read but had absolutely no interest in sitting down to read. As I reached the end of one of the bookshelves, I noticed a small table and chair set.

I sat down and opened the drawer of the table. In it were random photos and a very old looking photo book. Of course, nosy me had to rummage through it. Pictures of what I assumed were his parents. Old, faded and rough around the edges pictures.

I picked up one of the pictures and on the back, it read "Sammy, age 9". I looked at the picture more closely and it was Sam, awkward Sam, on a skateboard, smiling. His hair was disheveled and he was all arms and legs. I managed a smirk myself. He hadn't changed a bit. His smile was all there. He looked happy.

I put the picture back where I found it (okay well, where I think I found it), and kept snooping around in the drawer. There were envelopes, lots of them. These envelopes were all rubber banded together. Of course, I had to look to see what they were! I undid the rubber band, and opened the very top envelope. My heart sank.

Dear Sophia,

Today is the greatest day of my life. You found me today. I knew you were coming for me. The moment I laid my eyes on you, I knew my world would be different. I know you don't know me yet, but I need to get this day down on paper. Maybe one day, I can show this to you while we sit on our swing on our porch, reminiscing about the good old days. I'm 22 years old now, and will be 23 years old by the time my transition to Flesh Craver is completed. I will always do right by you. This is my promise to you. To give you the love and support you need to live in this crazy world. I am yours forever.

All my love,
Sam

The next envelope...

Dear Sophia,

It has been 3 months now and I do not think you notice me much. I know you are busy recruiting, so I will try to stay out of your way. I met Hannah today and bought you a real nice gift. It is a stone. This stone is special, you see. If used correctly, it can take you to a different realm, a realm that is restricted to Flesh Cravers. I have thought that maybe, if we found each other's hearts, we could use this stone together and live a happy life in this realm.

I have been doing a lot of reading and research to learn as much as I can to be the best I can be for you. I know you do not see that right now, but just you wait and see. You already have my heart. I will wait for the day you open yours up to me.

All my love,

Sam

The next envelope...

Dear Sophia,

It has now been 1 year since you found me. My transition into Flesh Craver is complete. I must say transitioning is no joke. The hunger hits you hard and fast and if you do not have the right orienter, things can go badly very quickly. Lucky for me, Adrian was good to me. She helped guide my first collection with grace and ease, and I collected without fail. I am so happy, only I wish I had shared that experience with you.

I do not know if you remember the day, but I came by your cubicle and asked you to come with me. You seemed distracted, sad almost. I wanted nothing more than to postpone my first collection and comfort you, but you told me to enjoy my collection and to come tell you all about it. Then you got up and walked away. Adrian told me recruiters do not typically take their recruit leads out on collections, but I was disappointed still. Reflectioning was scary the first time, but I handled it with ease (at least that is what Adrian said).

My experience in Reflection World showed me some pretty scary stuff (like my first signs of my Scenter genes coming out to play). I saw myself when I was 13, scared out of my mind, my eyes changing colors and my nostrils flaring. I could see every detail of my body, my hairs rising, goosebumps peeking out from under the first two layers of my skin. It scared me, yes, but it did not kill my spirit. It was that day that I started to work on my acceptance of being a Scenter.

I still have a long way to go, but hopefully, with you by my side, we can work on our issues together.

Until next time,

All my love,
Sam

I seriously could not read anymore. Well, didn't want to read anymore. But, I couldn't help it either. Had Sam kept all of these letters through all of these years, hoping to give them to me some day?

My first thought wanted to be "what a weirdo" but I couldn't consider it. That thought was pushed aside by sadness and a little bit of compassion. He had been waiting for me all these years. Slightly romantic. Slightly.

I fumbled through some of the many envelopes and opened one closer to the bottom. They seemed to be in the order he wrote them so it was interesting to see what a newer one would say. After all of these years of me treating him like crap, he has to have gotten over the mushy "all my love" stuff right?

Dear Sophia,

You met Jeremy today. I could have stopped it. I should have stopped it. I could have taken the case file instead of letting Evan give it to you. However, that would not have been fair to you. He was meant to be in your life. You were meant to meet and fall in love. Who am I to interfere with that? Even though I knew you were meant to meet, I never knew when it would happen. I didn't think it would happen this soon. I mean, it is really not that soon when you think about it, but too soon for me.

Too soon for you to not have realized my love for you. Too soon for me to not have proven myself to you. All of these years I have had to show you who I really am and what I am really capable of. To show you I can be that person that captures your heart. After all of these years, it is now clear to me that I have been, as you put it, that annoying little brother. Guess what? I don't want to be that annoying little brother. I want to be that amazing lover. That one and only. That person that you can't stop thinking of, day and night. I'm so disappointed in myself. I'm not angry with you and I'm sorry if I have recently shown a slightly different side of me to you. It's that ugly jealous side coming out. I have no issues with Jeremy. Except for the fact that he won you over in five minutes. I've been trying for forty years.

Know this. I will still be here for you. My love will stay true and I will wait. I have researched a lot and have asked some colleagues of mine to help me learn many things, things I'm not supposed to know so I can't even put them down on paper. I will be here, waiting for you. I can't say I won't start playing the field because forty years is a long time to wait, but I can say that no one will even have my heart as you do.

Waiting impatiently,
Sam

I didn't realize this, but I was crying. He knew Jeremy and I were going to meet and he had the power to stop it and didn't? Why wouldn't he be selfish and stop the encounter if he KNEW? Was he really that good of a guy? Was I really that blind and stupid?

Wait. Don't answer that question because I think I know the answer to it!

Here's the thing. I remember that day he went on his first collection. It was the same day I had finally heard from Max since we broke up. I was so upset and emotional. I didn't have time for a newly turned Flesh Craver in love with me. Did I know he was in love with me back then? Absolutely not. Did I care? Absolutely not. Do I feel bad for making him feel that way? Kinda.

I put all of the envelopes back together and neatly piled them back into the drawer. Sam would know I went through them. Oh well. Maybe he will bring it up, maybe not. I wasn't going to. All I wanted right now was to be in Jeremy's arms.

I searched high and low for a mirror. I know Reflectioning was not the right route to go, but I felt like a caged vandion in here. I wanted out! After I about tore the place apart looking for a mirror and not finding one, I slumped onto the chair and stared into space.

Think Sophia, think. How can you get out of here. Sam said if we used majick, we could be found. I didn't want to be found by those Drünods, but I wanted to be found by Jeremy. Was he looking for me? Did Hannah tell him I was okay? Hannah! I can call Hannah! If only I had a phone. That idea went right down the drain.

I immediately had one of the most brilliant ideas I have ever had. Call for Max! It's not majick. It's heavenly. It's natural. I closed my eyes and thought about Max. I screamed out for him in my mind. I opened my eyes and nothing. Enough was enough! Where was he?

"Maaaaaaaax," I yelled into the room.

"Please come find me. I need your help."

Nothing.

"Maaaaaax. Where are you?"

I noticed I had begun to cry again. I cried because I was afraid. I cried because I felt trapped. I cried because I was alone. Pacing the library room, I cried some more. I draped myself across the uncomfortable lounge chair and hugged the pillow. I cried myself to sleep.

My dreams were odd. I mean, like, crazy, weird, creepy odd. I was in a hospital on the Earth realm and was being "cared for" by humans. They had me strapped in a hospital bed and I was dressed in one of those awful hospital gowns that open in the back. I felt cold, exposed. There were brilliant bright lights coming from every which direction and it was really hard for me to focus on anything and anyone.

I saw doctors. I saw nurses. I saw

assistants. Lots of people, coming and going. At one point, a group of tourists came into my room and they were taking pictures of me. They were pointing and laughing; mumbling things like "look at her in that gown" and "I can't stop looking at her mouth."

I reached up to touch my mouth and realized that I had blood all over my mouth. It had hardened in most places and there were some chunks that were stuck to my chin. Someone brought a mirror to me and I got a really good look at myself. My face was covered in blood.

I looked down and realized my gown, the food tray, the walls, the floor – they were all covered in coagulated blood. I know I'm a Flesh Craver but sometimes, the sight of all of that blood makes me sick to my stomach, maybe some remnants of my human days. The group of tourists just pointed and laughed.

They laughed so hard it made my ears hurt. They snapped pictures with their bright flashes and all I could see were swirls of whites and light grays. A doctor came in and shooshed everyone out of the room and all went silent.

He walked up to me and had a warm rag in his hands. His mouth was covered with one of those face masks and he was wearing a bright green little doctor cap. I could only see his eyes. "Sophia, you must be exhausted. Let's get you all cleaned up and rested," he said. He placed the damp cloth on my mouth and wiped; he proceeded to clean all of the blood on my skin and called in a nurse to change my robe.

I finally regained most of my vision and noticed that my I.V. bag was filled with blood. The blood was flowing into my veins.

"Doctor?" I asked.

"Can I just have the bag of blood to drink?"

He held my hand in his and said "Sophia, I can't very well give you this bag of blood to drink. You're not a vampire. You're a Flesh Craver. Flesh Cravers must eat flesh. I can give you something better."

He walked over to a mini refrigerator and pulled something out. He held it behind his back as he walked over to me.

"Surprise, Sophia. We have all been waiting for this moment. I hope you enjoy this."

Instantly, camera crews, nurses, other patients, children – it seemed like the whole world was squeezing in my hospital room. I think I heard circus music playing over the intercom system and everyone was laughing. Dr. mysterious handed me what he had removed from the refrigerator and placed it in my hands. Immediately, camera flashes started going, I assume to capture the moment.

I could not see. I could only feel. It felt heavy. It felt wrong. I was so hungry. When did my arms get freed? My legs were still strapped in. With the lights, the circus music and the crowd, I tried to focus on what he had given me. All went silent. The lights dimmed. The curtains went down. The show was over. In my hands, I was holding…..

"Sophia! Sophia! Wake up!!"

I woke up to find Sam staring down at me, his eyes crazed with concern.

"Are you all right?" he asked. I was so not all right. I was disoriented. I was scared. I was cold. It took me a few minutes to realize I was no longer dreaming and Sam had wakened me from this horrifying dream.

Sam took his palm and wiped the tears that had been streaming down my face. I found it hard to breathe.

"Sophia, what the hell were you dreaming about? Did the dream creapers attack you?" What? What was he talking about? Who, or what the hell, are dream creapers?

As I sat up, Sam walked over to the table and brought me some smoothie flesh. I gulped it down as if I hadn't eaten in years. It instantly calmed me and I felt the blood rush back to my legs.

Good. I can move now. I walked over to him and sat at the table.

"Sam, I don't want to talk about my dream right now. Tell me, were you able to find anything out about what's going on?" I asked. He paced a while and kept smoothing out his hair. His footsteps sounded echoey and loud. I noticed his breathing was getting heavier and he seemed like he was about to lose it.

"Sam, what's wrong?" I asked.

Faster than I thought was possible, Sam raced over to me, picked me up and we were up on the second level of his secret room. He pushed me into a wall and stood directly in front of me. His right hand was placed firmly on my shoulder, pinning me to the wall. In his left hand, he held a sword. We stood there for a few seconds, and every heartbeat, every gasp, every whisper seemed to pierce through the loud silence of the room.

Sam's breathing became elevated, but quiet. I watched him; he was doing his Scenter thing. It really was unreal watching him in action. I never cared to learn about this side of Sam, but the more he showed it to me, the more fascinating it all seemed. Sam's nostrils worked on overdrive and I noticed the hairs on the back of his neck stand straight up.

The hairs on his arms were moving in small waves, trying to feel the threat. He held the sword directly in front of him and he held it like a warrior. I realized I had some flesh in my throat and was trying extremely hard not to cough.

It was tickling. It was getting annoying. I had no choice but to clear my throat. Sam quickly turned to me and looked directly into my eyes. His eyes had turned that grey color and they were beautiful. However, there was fear in his eyes. His posture changed, and he backed into me, pinning me even harder into the wall.

What was he doing? What did he hear? What did he smell? I thought nothing could get into this room. All of a sudden, I was afraid. Whatever was making Sam afraid, I mean, if SAM was afraid, it should only be logical that I be afraid too, right?

I was only a Flesh Craver. Sure, natural born Flesh Cravers have a lot more strength than turned Flesh Cravers, but Sam was also a Scenter/Flesh Craver. He was surely stronger than I was. And HE was afraid. My legs were buckling. I was shaking. Sam put his arm around me and we walked slowly towards a door. He placed his hand on one of the books on the bookshelf and it scanned his handprint. The door opened, and we stepped in.

As the door was automatically closing behind us, there were loud screeches approaching the opening. Sam guarded the door as it was closing. Was this door EVER going to close? It seemed to take forever, and it was just slow enough for me to see one Drünod floating really fast, almost like a ghost or phantasm, toward the opening. Sam held his sword in place and just as the door closed, Sam struck the Drünod on its cloaked arm and sliced right through. Its arm landed inside this new room and its body remained on the other side of the door.

15 SAM

We both stared at the wiggling arm on the floor for a few seconds. Sam, still holding the sword and me, still trying to stand on my own two feet. Sam walked over to the arm and gave it a small kick. The hand tried to grab his foot, but failed miserably.

Sam smirked, walked over to a cabinet, opened a drawer and got a box. He carried the box over and carefully placed the nasty arm in the box. He whispered an incantation and the box was sealed. Majick! We can finally get out of here!

"Sam, you did Majick! Can we PLEASE leave now? I'm really scared."

I almost screamed this out at him. He walked up to me, stood directly in front of me and I looked up. When did he get so tall? He was seriously towering over me.

"Sophia, look at me. Look at me. Look at my eyes."

As he said this, his eyes changed from brown to grey in an instant.

His breathing became deep and I think I heard a little growl. He took my hands and made me touch his arms, made me feel the goosebumps all over his arms and how his hairs were moving in that waving motion.

"Now, close your eyes," he said. I did. I didn't know what else to do. I felt like I was in some sort of trance. When I closed my eyes, Sam placed my palm over his heart. Thump thump. Thump thump. Thump thump. His heartbeat was a steady drum. He leaned in and whispered in my ear.

"Just feel, listen, concentrate."

When I let myself do just that, I felt taken aback by emotions. Loss. Fear. Hopelessness. Love. Laughter. Tension. I smelled every item in this room. The dusty book at the very top of the bookshelf and its musty smell. Sam's hair smelled of freshly cut firewood.

I heard the blood flowing through Sam's veins. The drumming of his heartbeat got louder the more I focused. This was nice. This was peaceful. I opened my eyes and broke the concentration. I found I had moved my ear onto Sam's chest. He had one strong arm around my waist and one arm across my shoulders. He had placed his chin on my head. His eyes had been closed, too.

As I began to pull away, I looked into Sam's eyes again, and again, they were that beautiful Scenter grey. Peaceful. His pupils were tiny pins in the center of his grey eyes, almost like a little galaxy existed within the universe of his eyes. He leaned down and just when I thought he would kiss me, because really, at this moment, I wanted him to, he simply gave me a kiss on my forehead.

"Sophia, welcome to my world. What you just experienced was a merging of two people, two energies. I let you in. I wanted you to feel me and feel how deep my love flows for you. All of this, my heartbeat, the smell of my hair, the look in my eyes, I allowed you to hear, to smell, to see. There is so much more where that came from. Now, I can find you, no matter where you are, and you can find me too."

And then, he turned his back to me.

I didn't know what to think. I didn't know what to feel. All of those feelings took over my entire body. It was as if I were in a new world. When we stood there for that period of time, I felt safe, warm. I felt as if the whole world could crumble around us and even still, it would all be okay. It was Sam's world. And he had let me in.

"Sam, why did you do that?" I asked. "Why did you let me in to your world?"

He sat down on a small cushiony chair at the end of the room and relaxed. I could still smell his firewood hair, could taste the sweet sweat on his flesh. He watched me walk over to the other chair as I sat down, still staring at him, waiting for an answer. He remained silent.

Dammit Sam! Why are you playing with my head? Why now? Sure, you had a gazillion years to prove yourself to me, and you choose NOW? Ugh, men. Always at the wrong place at the most definitely wrong time. He still wasn't answering me and we just sat there, staring at each other.

After a few minutes of playing the staring game, Sam opened his mouth.

"Did you want to kiss me?" he asked.

Huh? This is the question he asks me? If I wanted to kiss him? I was so not going to answer this question, mainly because I didn't want to tell him the answer. But then again, he already knew the answer. Damn these Scenters!

"Yes, Sam. Yes, I wanted to kiss you. It

was a romantic moment. It was surreal. Is that what you want to hear?" I asked, clearly agitated.

I hated when people placed me in situations like these. He knew how I would answer and he knew damn well what that moment would do to me.

"Sophia, ask me why I didn't try to kiss you."

"All right Sam. Humor me. Why didn't you try to kiss me?" I asked.

He looked away and smiled.

"Because when we kiss for the first time, I want to know that you are mine and I am yours. I want you to be so in love with me that I am the only person you will ever want to kiss and hold. I want to be the only person you dream of and the only person you want to wake up next to every day. I want us to experience the world together and I don't want to kiss you when we have a majickal moment. I want to kiss you when you feel my heart and love are the only majick you need."

After careful consideration of the trillion choice words I wanted to spew out at him, I said "fair enough."

I didn't have time for this. If he was trying to prove something, now wasn't the right time. So what. Now he thinks he can majickally make me fall for him? Sure. This Scenter stuff is pretty cool and this merging of two people was really romantic and awesome. But, my heart strings were with Jeremy.

As much as Sam was trying, he just could not accept the fact that he was not the one for me. He was just trying too hard.

He must have felt a shift in my mood because

his entire demeanor changed. He stood up and I finally paid enough attention to my surroundings. This smaller room branched off the larger library. It was still a nice size, just not as impressive. It was again lined with bookshelves and neat little lanterns strewn about here and there creating that pretty glow of dancing shadows on the walls. Sam pulled a drape and unmasked a beautiful mirror. I had never been so happy to see a mirror in all my life!

"Sophia, the Drünods found us because you called for Max. You shouldn't have done that. I told you you were safe here, with me, and I would protect you. Why don't you believe me?" He seemed sad. Disappointed. I opened my mouth to try to redeem myself and he stopped me.

"Don't say anything Sophia. You know, it's really bad when you can't trust me, ME, after all I have done for you throughout the years and I have never done you harm or wrong. You have to be so desperate and too afraid and call to your Angel ex-boyfriend to come to your rescue. Have you ever thought that the protection spell I placed in here was a protection spell from anything and everything? Even Angels?"

"You know, not all Angels are good. I was prepared to stick up for you and protect you against all of this evil surrounding, well, YOU. You are the target, not me. Not Jeremy. Not Hannah. And not Max. It's you. Did YOU ever consider why we are all here to help you? Did YOU ever consider why it was decided I would be the best person to protect you and keep you safe? Of course not. Why? Because you are so wrapped up in your little idealistic world with Jeremy that you aren't open to the possibility that he may be the one who is causing you harm. Have you thought about when all of this started happening to you? Was it before or after you recruited him?"

Sam huffed, nostrils flared, took my hand and we were off into Reflection World. He didn't even give me a moment to argue with him. The images I saw were like none I had ever seen before. Mountains, big and small. Valleys and streams. Deep nature colors. Sam everywhere.

A small house in the fields. Butterflies the size of ravens fluttering by. Wolves in packs, protecting their territory – the house. Sam, standing on a cliff, sniffing the air. Smiling. Happy. I could smell nature all over. The sap in the trees. The damp leaves. The moss on the rocks. The sky was a magnificent view of dusk. You could see planets off in the distant galaxies. What plane were we on in this scene?

As quickly as I felt relaxed, we were immediately rushed back to reality to the offices of F.L.E.S.H. Evan was waiting for us on the other side and had three very large men lead me away from Sam. Sam was fighting to stay with me, but they tore us apart. Sam was fighting, struggling to break free from what I could see of at least six men holding him down.

Evan had a strange look on his face. I screamed for Sam as I watched them beat him down to the floor – I saw blood, lots of blood. They dragged me away into an elevator and Sam looked up at me just enough for us to make eye contact. I could hear him in my mind "I will find you" and someone kicked him in the face, causing him to fall unconscious.

"Where are you taking me?" I asked.

These men were strong. They held onto my arms so hard I know for sure I would have bruises, even if they only lasted for a few hours. I had no idea who they were. Evan was looking away from me and avoiding my questions. I continued to squirm and wiggle from these men, but I wasn't going anywhere. They were too strong. I tried to bite one of them but he growled at me. Oh. A fellow Scenter. I see. Now they were playing dirty. Where were they taking me?

We exited the elevator and walked through dark tunnels. I swear with all of the majick in the world at our fingertips, F.L.E.S.H. still relied on stupid fire lanterns for lighting. It was dark. It was creepy. And, I was pretty sure there were insects crawling on me and rodents creeping away in the shadows. The ground was damp, almost splashy. My ankles were getting soaked and my once really pretty skirt was almost drenched in watery stinkiness.

Were we in sewers? I've heard horror stories of the Pleasers that live down here and attack force feed Flesh Cravers during their travels.

"Evan, what's going on? Why won't you talk to me?" I pleaded. Again, he didn't answer.

"Maaaaaxxxx" I yelled.

At once, one of the men holding onto me placed his hand firmly over my mouth.

"Uh, uh, uh" he said. "You must be silent. No calling your Angel."

Where was Max? Why couldn't he hear me? I closed my eyes and thought of Max. He should be able to feel me in distress, right? Like he said, if I was thinking about him enough, he would come to me. I tightened my eyes, stumbling over my feet as I was being dragged down these tunnels, and thought of Max.

Max, please help. Max, if you can feel me, I need you more than ever. Please, come help me. The three men holding me were now digging their nails into my flesh. I felt some blood trickling down my arm, cool and warm blood. I felt my hunger begin to build.

I opened my eyes after a few minutes, having given up completely on Max saving me. The man with the hand over my mouth gave up as well when he realized I had lost most of my energy and they were basically dragging me to wherever they were taking me.

Evan walked ahead of us, stone faced and silent. We turned a corner and entered a room. The steel door shut behind us and the men threw me onto the floor. Cold, metal floor thank you very much. Jerks.

As soon as I got up, Evan walked over to me and pointed up to the ceiling.

"See that Sophia? That is a row of cameras. We have this place heavily secured with surveillance cameras to watch over you and protect you. These three gentlemen here are your guards. This here is Marco. Over here to your left is Lucas. And over to your right is Brad. As I said, they are here to protect you. You need anything, just ask them. But really, don't waste your time asking them what's going on, where you are and what's happening. It will do you no good. Sweet Hiliad, Sophia! Why didn't you come to us when you were first in trouble? We could have helped you a lot sooner than now. You know we take care of our own. What were you thinking?"

Evan said these words as if he were my

father, lathered in disappointment and disgrace. I didn't know what to say as usual. What? Should I have said 'Evan, I was being selfish and didn't want you to know all of this stuff because I didn't want you to think I had caused it' or 'Evan, I don't know what's happening but I was too stubborn to ask for your help'. Either way, I would have sounded like a stupid little kid and he had every right to speak to me this way. Why DIDN'T I come to him for help?

"Evan, please please please just tell me where everyone is and that everyone is okay. Where is Jeremy? Why were those men beating Sam?"

Evan turned quickly in my direction and his face completely changed.

"Sophia, you don't know what's going on and the less you know right now, the better. You stay here with the guys while we figure this out for you. Let me handle this." Evan walked out and the door slammed shut behind him.

Lucas, Marco and Brad stepped in front of the door with their arms crossed over their extremely muscular chests. They too were stone-faced, almost like statues. I walked around the room to see what was available to me. Metal walls, metal tables and chairs, metal everything. Couldn't they at least make me comfortable? From overhead, I heard Evan's voice.

"Sophia, to the left of the room there is a table. On that table is a microphone. If you need something just speak into the microphone and we will accommodate. Let us know when you are hungry."

There was a screeching sound as the mic on his end switched off. I ran over to the microphone and clicked the little button.

"Evan, I want to talk to Sam," I said. I got no reply. Hey, I had to try.

As I sat on the small cot with no cushion or pillows, I tried to make sense of all of this in my head. Sam had been right. None of this started happening to me until I recruited Jeremy. When did I start seeing the Drünods? Think Sophia think. It was in Reflection World and we were traveling after recruiting Netasha. Netasha! Wait. Were they after Netasha?

I totally forgot about her. I had to tell Evan. No. I can't tell him. I have to talk to Sam. He seemed to know more than he was telling me and I needed a way to get to him. I closed my eyes and remembered what Sam had told me. Now he could find me, and I could find him too. I pictured Sam. Smelled his hair. Felt his heartbeat. Sam. Can you hear me? Are you okay?

Sure enough, Sam was in my mind.

"Sophia, I can hear you. I am okay. They have me in a holding cell. I don't know why they are holding me, they won't talk. They have so many guards around me there's no way I can fight them off. Do you know where you are?"

I tried to explain to him where I was dragged, but couldn't say how many turns we made because I was busy calling for and thinking of Max and I didn't want him to have a fit again. Sam was also dragged through some watery tunnels so we figured we were somewhat close to each other. Sam spoke to me again. "I will figure something out. In the meantime, stay calm and don't do anything stupid" he huffed. I was glad he was safe and they hadn't hurt him too badly.

I went over to the microphone and asked for some food. I had felt my hunger appear while I was dragged through the tunnels, and if Sam and I were going to make a break for it, I really needed to be in full strength. A few minutes later, the guards let a volunteer through the door so that I could feed.

I smelled her a mile away and all of my other thoughts left me. I was starving. I raced over to her and in a swoop bit down into her neck. She yelped a little but I was so engrossed in the collection I didn't care. I gnawed. I chewed and I sucked. I felt blood pouring down my face in streams, and I bit down again.

I was in my own feeding world and it wasn't until the guards had to pull the volunteer away from me that I realized I was killing her. When I looked her way, I saw I had bitten so many places of her body and ripped off so much of her flesh she was bleeding badly and I had not recited the spell.

She was convulsing and the guards had to lay her on the floor and heal her. Lucas seemed to have his majick at his fingertips and healed her wounds immediately. She raced over to the door and ran out quickly, sobbing in fear.

Marco came over to me and handed me a damp towel. I wiped the blood off of me in embarrassment. He looked down at me with judgy eyes and a frown on his face. Why was my hunger so out of control? I called out to Sam again.

"Sam, I just fed and I almost killed the girl. I don't know what's happening to me and why my hunger is so wacky, but we need to get out of here. Evan isn't explaining anything and I am scared. Do you know what's keeping the Drünods away?"

It took a few seconds for Sam to answer, but he finally did.

"They performed some sort of ritual outside of my cell and I'm sure they did the same for you. I heard only parts of the ritual, but I think that's what is keeping them out. Don't worry Sophia. Remember what I told you. I am here for you and I will fix this. Why don't you get some rest and when you wake up, hopefully I will have some more answers."

I lay down on the super cold and horribly uncomfortable cot. I closed my eyes and sleep found me. It found me quickly. It found me easily. I was full and exhausted. I fell asleep thinking of Jeremy. Cecily. Hannah. Max. Netasha. Sam. Not in that order.

My dreams were disoriented images of nothing and everything. It was like being in Reflection World with a thousand beings and seeing all of their stories combined into one scene. Drünods, dancing Mallies, wolf packs, beautiful non-existent Angel wife. A loud crashing sound woke me from my sleep and I fell off the cot onto the floor.

Getting my glasses back on and trying to focus on what was happening around me was fun. It was dark. Stupid fire lanterns made the room look like there were a million ghastly dark figures dancing around, waiting to strike. Marco, Lucas and Brad were pacing the room, looking around for where the loud crashes were coming from.

Still, there was always one of them guarding the door. The loud crashes continued and it sounded like something was trying to get in. From the overhead speakers, I could hear Evan yelling, "breach in security fellas, time to move." As soon as they heard that, Lucas grabbed my arm and whisked me away toward the door. Ouch! Why did he have to be so rough?

This time, I was ready to watch. To listen. To smell.

"Sam, can you hear the commotion?" I asked, hoping he would hear me. He did.

"Yeah, what's going on out there?" he asked.

"I don't know. All I know is that Evan said there was a security breach and my three security guards dragged me out of my cell. Are they moving you?" He paused for a second and said he was trying to hear what they were saying but they were too far away for him to hear. He did feel something powerful though.

"Sophia, I feel a really strong energy. I can't quite get the scent yet, but it's extremely strong. Let me know where they are taking you. I have to try to figure out a way to get out of here and find you."

The crashing sounds grew louder and it seemed as if we were being followed by them. I won't lie, I was scared. Even my security guards weren't making me feel safe enough. They were moving faster. My feet were once again being dragged – they may as well have carried me if I was slowing them down. My one shoe fell off and splashed behind us somewhere.

"Hey!" I yelled.

"Slow down." Lucas just looked at me and growled.

"Hurry up if you want to live," he said.

"Alright fellas, enough is enough. We are Flesh Cravers. It's extremely hard to kill us.

Why are we so afraid?"

As soon as I said that, the dim halls lit up with a brilliant ultra-white flash and sounds like crashing thunder rocked the walls and floors. We fell, and they lost their grip on me. I took the opportunity and ran. I ran up and down the halls. I turned corner after corner.

I heard them screaming as the crashing and flashing grew louder behind me. Whatever it was, it was coming after me. I had no idea where I was or how I was going to get out of here.

"Sophia, can you hear me?"

Sam called out to me. Only, it wasn't in my head. He was close.

"Sophia, I can smell you! You are close to my cell. Hurry. It's getting closer."

I ran as fast as I could and stumbled on my one remaining shoe. I kicked it off and regained my balance. I ran faster. Before I knew it, I was in a very narrow hallway, surrounded by cells. I could smell fresh firewood and knew Sam was close. As I inched down the hallway, the sounds and flashing behind me were so close I could feel it.

Every time I turned back, I could see lanterns cutting out and darkness. Then a flash. Then darkness. Within the cells, I saw all kinds of beings. Fire demons. Fairies. Shadow demons. Pleasers. Vampires. Poltergeists. Werewolves. They were pacing their cells; they knew something was going on, and were equally as disturbed as I was.

I finally reached Sam and he ran up to the bars.

"You found me. Quick, help me break out of this cell."

I stared at him, clearly lost. Hey, if I had known how to break out of a cell, I would have broken out of my own.

"Sam, um, how are we going to do that?" I asked. He smirked.

"Together" he said.

We held hands and we were merged again. Sam whispered in my ear to think of never letting anything separate us. To think of these bars not being here. To give us the strength to break through the barriers. I felt heat rising inside me, I felt my heartbeat increase to match his and together, we held onto the bars of the cell.

He let out a deep growl and when I looked into his eyes, I could see my reflection in them. My eyes had turned the same pale grey as his. Together, we tore the bars apart and dissipated any majick that had been cast on them.

"See, wasn't that amazing?" Sam asked.

He was smiling and looked so smug. I was going to say something snide and snarky, but I didn't want to ruin the moment for him. For us. It was pretty freaking amazing!

He held my hand and we ran. He knew where he was going. The crashing and lightning was behind us, getting closer and closer. As we flew up and down the hallways, twisting and turning every which way, Sam kept looking back and moved faster. He was taking long strides and we seemed to almost float with his every step. Suddenly, he stopped. It all happened in slow motion and my craver reflexes weren't fast enough. Directly behind us all went black. All was still.

Directly ahead of us, the fire lanterns dimmed until they went out with a poof. We were in darkness. Sam held me into his chest and I could hear his breathing change. He was sniffing. His heart slowed. He was listening. We stood there, in complete and utter darkness, for what seemed like years. A brilliant light appeared and the all too familiar glow of the heavenly dawn was showering us.

There was Max, wings displayed and floating down the hall towards us. Sam firmed his grip on me. Max landed with grace onto the damp floor of the tunnel and looked around. In a whisper, all lanterns were lit and the air was warm. He walked over to us and placed one hand on Sam's shoulder. Sam raised his hand and pulled me away.

"Stand back Angel. Serminian Angels do not cause destruction as we saw back there. How many did you kill?" he said with disgust. Angels – another one of those sneaky things that can actually kill a Flesh Craver.

Max looked down and shed a golden Angelic tear.

"I didn't come to destroy or kill. It was not my intention. These beings are causing havoc within the realms and I feel a personal obligation to help. When I heard Sophia's cries, I tried to get to her. No thanks to your spell, I couldn't get in to save the two of you from the Drünods. I have been trying to help Sophia for the past several days. I have heard her cries for me. I have felt her fear. I needed to help. We need to go quickly and I can explain more." He draped his wings over all three of us and transported us to his plane. Heaven? Seriously?

16 THE REALMS ARE FALLING APART

When we arrived, Heaven wasn't all I thought it would be. It was normal. It was plain. Sure, there was a "glow" to the place. Sure, things smelled much nicer, like all of the flowers and the grass and the trees. The air was clear and free of those earthly and other realmly toxins. It was nice. But definitely not what I would expect to see for it being Heaven. I actually didn't know what I should have expected.

Max sat us down on the grass as he stood and paced. He kept running his hand into his hair and seemed anxious, nervous.

"Listen up Sophia and Sam. We do not have much time. These things are out for blood. Sophia. Your blood. There are hundreds of them on the prowl for you. They have directives to hunt and return. They do not plan to kill you, at least not yet. They need you for something."

"Better yet, whoever is ordering them around needs you. Whatever the case is, this person is strong. They are powerful and know most of the tricks of the trade. The only thing I can think of is to get back into the F.L.E.S.H. cave archives and try to find some more answers in the cave drawings."

As he was talking, I was only half listening.

"Can we please find Jeremy and Hannah, please?" I pleaded. I didn't want to do anything else until I knew they were all right and here with me.

"I mean, don't we have more power if we are together. Hannah has so much knowledge and she's a siren. She has special powers too. I'm sure she can help us."

I thought for sure this would get them to listen to me. I know Jeremy is still human, but I really needed him here. I needed him holding me and I really needed his comfort.

Max spoke with dismay.

"Sophia, Jeremy, Cecily and Hannah were abducted and we don't know where they are. Evan was trying to keep you in the cell until he found some answers but I really needed to get you out of there. The Drünods were coming for you, and even Evan does not have the best of the best of spells to keep them away. There are just too many of them. I can help; I just need some more resources."

Sam and I looked at each other. I'm glad Sam spoke first.

"Max, buddy, pal. Can't you just call on some of your other Angelic colleagues to help us out? You clearly have some strength and power and we could use all the help we can get."

Max looked away.

"I am not able to ask for help. This is not a holy mission, but a personal one. I am not allowed to place my colleagues in harm's way for personal business matters."

"I was already scolded for doing as much as I have done. I must finish this and return to my missions."

"Then let me out of here Max" said Sam.

"I don't want to be here wasting time. We need to get back to The Lost Petals and deal with this. I'm tired of running and hiding."

Sam punched a tree and the trunk cracked in half. The tree came tumbling down with force and might. Max guided the tree back up with his light and healed it back together.

"Sam, don't destroy things here. Control whatever animalistic beast you have inside of you and calm down. You can't go back without a plan."

Sam glared at him with contempt. He hated when people referred to him as an animal, and Max knew that. Max was right. We needed a plan. I felt like a helpless twelve year old that needed protecting. I wanted to help. After all, they were after me and all of this was to save me. Right?

"Max, what can I do to help? Just say the word and I can do it." I said.

Max thought for a minute and said, "Can you get into the caves without looking suspicious?" I laughed.

"Of course I can. I know the head cavearian there. Old family friend. I've been to the caves plenty of times to research."

I didn't say this, but sight-see was more like it.

"I can get in, no problem." Sam stood next to me and asked, "can you get me in with you? You're not going alone you know." Of course. How could I forget? I needed a babysitter.

It was settled. Max would take us back to F.L.E.S.H. and we formulated a plan in which he would distract Evan to give us enough time to get to the caves and try to get some more answers. What no one knew yet was that I had a plan of my very own.

Max hovered over us with his beautiful silky wings and we ended up inside the F.L.E.S.H. library. The knowledge fairies danced their way over to us just as Max disappeared.

"May we help you?" they asked, collectively, smiling. Ugh! I don't know how they could be so clueless as to what was going on around them and they were always so freaking happy! It really was sickening.

"Um, no, we are just waiting for a friend," I muttered. They hovered for a moment and breezed past us.

Sam stood beside me, taking advantage of every moment to touch me in some way. Put his arm across my shoulders. Hold my elbow. I can't say either way how I felt about this, but I can say all I wanted was to find Jeremy. Was Max right? Were he, Cecily and Hannah abducted? How did he know this?

As Sam and I made our way through the halls of F.L.E.S.H., I could not figure out how I could ditch him. Yeah, I felt safer with him, yeah he had some more qualities than I had to feel, hear and smell fear and whatnot, but he wasn't doing anything to try to help me find the people I cared about. Sure, it was important to find out why these Drünods were coming after me and what was happening to me with my hunger going all crazy, but still, I wanted my friends, AND my boyfriend!

Sam was almost suffocating me with protection. I had an idea.

"Sam, I have to go to the bathroom. Do you mind?" I asked. He frowned.

"I'm coming with you," he said.

I laughed so hard he looked at me as if I was some sort of Bulginian Nedan. You know, the creatures that have seven elongated heads and five perfectly placed eyes in each head?

"Um, no, you're not," I snapped.

"Sophia, there are a ton of mirrors in these restrooms. You can't possibly think I am going to let you go in by yourself right?" I had to think. Quick.

"Sam, let me go to the bathroom in peace. I cannot use the bathroom with someone hovering over me. It doesn't work that way!"

Yeah, I was sounding whiney, but sweet Goddess Hiliad, I just wanted to use the bathroom!

"Two minutes. That is all you get. Two minutes. If you are not out by then, I am coming in to get you. Do not try anything stupid, and absolutely do not Reflection! I swear Sophia. I can feel your intentions. You're up to no good. Knock it off and just listen to me for a change."

He looked angry and frustrated. Yes! Some alone time. I nodded and busted my way into the restroom. I closed the stall behind me and called for Melody.

"Melody" I whispered.

"Melody, can you hear me. Please, I need your help." I summoned some mist for her and she instantly appeared. Before she could say one word, I shushed her.

"You have to be really quiet. I need your help real bad. Do you remember Sam, the person I work with that is completely obsessed with me? He is waiting outside this bathroom door and he is going to come in any minute now. He is stalking me and I need to escape him. I can't Reflection right now because there's some really creepy stuff happening in Reflection World, but I need you to do me a huge favor."

Melody nodded her head in agreement and floated up and down with joy. "Sophia, I am so happy I can help my bestest friend. What do you need?"

After we worked out all of the details in about fifteen horrifyingly long seconds, Melody was ready. I conjured enough mist for her to get into the hallway just as I opened the door.

"What the?"

Sam gasped. He did not have time to finish. Melody swarmed him with her misty greatness and blinded him.

She swirled all around him, confusing him, making his senses go berserk.

"Hi Sam. Sophia tells me you want to date her. You know, I am her best friend and I need to approve of any guy she's with. Let's see now, tell me all about yourself."

Melody went on and on, as any teenager would, asking him a million questions, all the while floating and hovering around him in fast circles and swoops. He could not break away.

I looked back to see Sam stumble on his own feet and fall, hard, on the floor. I ran. I ran as fast as I could to lose him. I made it to the elevator and was instantly zipped down to the first floor, directly in front of the entrance and exit to F.L.E.S.H. I needed some majick, and I needed it now.

I quickly walked through the darkened streets of The Lost Petals. Every sound, every whisper, every creak, scared me silly. I hunched over and was nearing Pleasers Alley. Their moans, cries and outstretched desperate arms were frightening.

There was a lot of foot traffic tonight.
Many beings out and about, walking to and
from. Since I was not paying attention to my
surroundings, just trying to avoid gross
Pleasers, I managed to run right into someone
and that being knocked me directly into
Pleaser's Alley. Pleasers leaped up and
surrounded me.

I could see them up close and personal now.
They were only human, true. Nevertheless,
there were a lot of them. Hundreds, maybe
thousands. Suddenly, I was drenched with
blood. Pleasers were cutting themselves to
feed me. They crawled down to me. They were
forcing their arms, fingers and toes, along
with every imaginable body part, into my
mouth, to feed me. Gurgling, sucking sounds
were playing in surround sound all over me.

My hunger was growing stronger by the
second. I could feel the need to collect
rising inside of me and in an instant, I knew
the moment was coming in which I could no
longer control it. I bit down. I fed. I was in
momentary bliss. The gummy flesh, some of it
covered in maggots and flies, was delicious.
The blood poured down my chin, my neck and my
arms in a sea of red waterfalls. I felt my
eyes roll back and I threw myself into the
collection. The Pleasers were getting very
loud now with their grunts and groans, but I
heard them from a distance.

I found myself in an almost dreamlike state. I
saw myself from above, a few dozen Pleasers
surrounding me and me, collecting from them in a
ravenous display of wild hunger. Veins were spewing
miniature fountains of crimson yumminess as I bit
down harder. Some of the Pleasers were
bleeding to death, and some had already died

with smiles on their faces. The Pleasers that
wanted to feed me tossed the ones that were
dead away like trash. They were crazed. I was
crazed. I felt my hunger grow stronger the
more I fed. Every bite, every chunk of flesh,
felt like bliss. I could not stop. I did not
want to stop.

As I watched myself bathe in flesh and
blood, a little voice in the back of my mind
spoke.

"Sophia, where are you?"

It was Sam.

"Why did you run from me? I sense you are
happy right now, but I cannot smell you. Tell
me where you are so that I can get you and we
can finish this investigation."

Sam, always so worried about the little
things. The little things. Wait. Sophia! What
was happening? I let the hunger take control.
I was in Pleaser's Alley. I killed humans. I
was enjoying it. No. This was not part of my
plan.

Engrossed in my hunger, I fought within
myself to find the stable, sane me. Yes, there
is such a part. As much as I wanted to live
here forever, collecting and bathing in soft,
gummy, bloody flesh, I knew I had to leave.
With every bit of inner strength I had left in
me, I clawed my was from the Pleasers grips,
tearing more flesh in a sad attempt to escape.
I concentrated on my Craver survival instincts
and thrust upward, soaring above the Pleasers,
and clung to the side of a building.

I held on to a lamppost and through
whitened eyes, watched them hurl themselves
into the building, trying to get to me. They
were getting smarter. They started to pile up
the dead bodies and climb them. I scaled the

building in my crazed hunger, barely able to see them since my eyes were still rolled into the back of my head and all was a whitish haze.

I reached the top of the building and threw myself on the roof. I lay there for a few minutes, calming down and finally felt my eyes come back to me. My breathing had steadied and I was feeling like myself again. Once I felt well enough to stand up, I felt all anxiety leave me. I was satisfied. I was full. I was ready to rule the world.

I ignored Sam's constant pleas to get me to tell him where I was. I raced over to my apartment and shut the door behind me. I was home. Great Goddess Hiliad I was home. It felt like years had passed since I had been here. I turned every light on and went into the bathroom. What I saw in the mirror made my skin crawl.

I was covered. I was covered in blood, flesh, and maggots and flies were swarming all around me. I had coagulated blood in my ears and in my nose. Any Flesh Craver can tell you, when we go on a collection, for the first several years while you learn to control the hunger, it can get somewhat messy. What I was, standing in front of this mirror at this moment, was beyond messy. It was downright hideous.

My chest had a slight mark; a burn mark from my Craver necklace. I had finally been so engrossed in my hunger – had gone so deep for the Craving, that my necklace heated up like a hot coal and branded me.

I turned the shower to scalding hot water and washed it all away. From time to time, I had to remove bits of flesh that fell off me from the drain to unclog it. It had started collecting and blocking the red and pink water from washing away. The urge to eat the discarded, soapy flesh was unbearable. I took my time showering. I scrubbed and scrubbed, and I cried. I cried because I was scared. I cried because I did not know where Jeremy was. I cried because I felt helpless. I cried because I felt weak.

After my moment of patheticness, I finished washing up and got dressed. I lay down on my bed and closed my eyes. I was so exhausted, I didn't have time to think I was in danger this entire time from the Drünods, and I fell asleep.

Sleep wasn't restful, but came easily and I snuggled up with my blanket and wandered off into dream world. Again, not part of my brilliant plan, but the insanity of my hunger had consumed me and had me to the point of delicious fleshy exhaustion.

In my dreams, I replayed the hospital bed scene. The doctors, the nurses, the tourists with their flashy cameras and brilliant white lights. Me, covered in blood, tied down to the hospital bed.

Circus music playing in full blast from every speaker in the room and all over the hospital. People were dancing. People were juggling body parts, and with each juggle, they managed to tear some flesh off and eat, not losing the rhythm of the juggle.

The doctor approached me again, and again, he handed me something from the refrigerator. I closed my eyes because in this scene, I did not want to replay what I was handed the last time I had this dream. I did not want to see it. I did not want to hold it again. However, no matter what I tried to do in my dream, it did not work. I was forced to relive this nightmare, and as I looked down to see what I was holding, I gasped in horror to see Jeremy's severed head in my hands.

His eyes were blankly staring back at me. I screamed for someone to help me. I still held Jeremy's head in my hands, refusing to let him go. This might sound gross and macabre to you, but imagine how you would feel holding the one you love in your hands, dead, even if it is their dead head? Okay, don't imagine that. It sounds wrong, but in my dream, I just couldn't put him down.

As I cried and screamed, the circus music got louder. The room was crowded, not an inch of space for anyone else to fit. People were rejoicing and carrying on with fireworks and confetti. I swear I thought I saw a piñata somewhere. In an instant, all was silent and I looked down at Jeremy's head. His mouth was moving.

I leaned in, and he whispered, "I had a vision this would happen, but I didn't believe it. I couldn't change it. I'm sorry I let you down Sophia." He gurgled up blood and it came spewing out of his mouth, all over my face.

"Know I will always love you and we will meet again in another life."

As he said this, his eyes closed and his light was gone.

I woke up. I was sweating all over and I wiped tears from my eyes. I know this was just a dream, but it had felt so real. Was this dream a vision of my own? Was I going to rip Jeremy's head off? No. Even if this wasn't a vision and just a weird paranoid I'm scared dream, I had to figure this out and I had to do it now!

I leaped out of bed and scaled my bookshelf. Majick spells book, where are you? I was so horrible with my majick. I never really remembered the spells that truly mattered. If only I could go back to Sam's and check out his collection of books. I should have thought of this when he left me alone all that time. Stupid stupid girl.

I needed a locator spell to find Cecily, Jeremy and Hannah. After searching for about ten minutes, I finally found the book I needed. Another fifteen minutes and I found my spell. When performing majick you had to be calm, relaxed, and confident - I was none of these right now. I recited anyway.

"In times of desperate need I beg your helping hand. What is lost can now be found with infinite demand. Please guide me to my lost friends in my time of need. Show me the way in vision form, this of you I plead."

Once I recited the spell, I was taken into a journey in my mind. I was taken under water, deep inside a purple ocean. I wasn't quite sure the location of this ocean but I swam with garrids and mermaids. The mermaids pointed toward an underwater cliff where there was a cave. I traveled into the cave and passed other foreign creatures. Some with fins so beautiful my heart skipped a few beats.

Others were creepy, almost hybrid like. Some of these creatures had noses where their ears should technically be and others had webbed eyelashes so long they looked like they could snatch you right into their web.

As I swam past these obscurities, I came to a narrow hall in the cave and saw cages on either side. Inside one of these cages, I saw a pleaser. There must have been majick placed on the outside of the cage so that the pleaser could still have oxygen. The pleaser was trying to claw its way out, grunting and moaning saying it needed to give up its flesh or it would die.

In another cage, I saw a Knowledge Fairy, sitting on a stool with one book in her hand, looking very sad. I came to the last cage and there was Cecily. She was tied up in what looked like those weird creatures' eyelashes or spider webs. Her once long beautiful hair had been cut to just above her pointed ears and she was crying.

I was immediately drawn backwards through the cave, past the Fairy, past the pleaser, past the creepy and beautiful creatures. Back up the purple ocean water and I splashed out. I got only a quick glance at my surroundings and was whipped back into my mind in my apartment. I was a bit dizzy for a moment but quickly gathered myself. Galariyan Oceans. That's what I read on the sign. Where WAS this place?

I grabbed a backpack, put my majick book and a change of clothes in and ran off to Hannah's store. As I rushed past Pleasers Alley, I couldn't help but notice the number of Pleasers there. They had about doubled since I had been trapped in there. Not paying attention to where I was looking I ran right into someone in quite the hurry.

"Well look who decided to show herself," said Sam. Here we go.

"Sam, I'm in a hurry right now so if you're with me, then you're with me. If not, you need to leave me be and let me find my friends."

He glanced over my shoulder, to either side of me and seemed to relax. I continued to walk in a hurry.

"Oh no. You are not ditching me again. I am coming with you. Goddess Sophia, why are you giving me such a hard time? I'm trying to help you."

After careful consideration, I thought why not? He's a Scenter. He can help weed out the bad people on our way.

"Fine. This is how you can help me. Will you Reflection with me to Galariyan Oceans? I am afraid to Reflection on my own for the obvious reasons."

His eyes lit up and he just about yelled "Yes of course I will. I'm in it until the end," was his answer.

So no need to go to Hannah's to find a map to the Galariyan Oceans and alternate ways of getting there. Hooray!

He held my hand, took out his pocket mirror and we were off into Reflection World. Drünods were standing by waiting for me but Sam quickly whisked me down the path to our exit. We were in Galariyan Oceans in no time. The Drünods could not follow. We saw them trapped within Sam's pocket mirror. He closed it shut.

As we walked down the lavender sands beach, Sam turned to me. He, with no words, held out his hand so that I could hold it.

"Stay close to me. This place is more dangerous than it seems."

If this was a ploy for him to get close to me I swear…

"Sam listen. I think they are all in a lot of trouble and I am going to need your help to help them. They are in an underwater cave somewhere here. I brought my spell book with me…"

Sam cut me off and said, "I know where they

are."

He recited a spell under his breath and before I knew it, we were in the water. I immediately fought because, hello, I can't swim!

Somehow, the fantastic spell Sam cast allowed me to breathe underwater. Don't know how, he just did it. He held my hand and we followed the mermaids as we swam down towards the cave. Before we entered, he looked at me and tightened his grip on my hand. I think he was enjoying this way too much. As we entered the cave, he must have whispered a spell to block the cave entrance and immediately I could breathe air. I choked a little on the water but overall it wasn't as traumatic as I initially thought it would be.

The entrance of the cave was exactly as my trip from the spell. I saw everything all over again, and just as vividly too. The eyelash creature lashed out at us as we walked past but luckily I knew it would be there and quickly moved out of its way before it got us.

As we passed the pleaser, he moaned and writhed in pain, begging us to let him feed us. He was covered in his own filth and blood oozed from his arm where he was missing a chunk of flesh. I felt a little pang of hunger strike up within me and I moved closer to the pleaser. Sam flinched and pulled me back.

"Sophia, what's wrong with you? Don't go near that pleaser!"

I mumbled something under my breath and all that got me was a nostril flare and growl from Sam.

We got to the end of the cave hall and reached Cecily. Poor Cecily - she was so vulnerable and weak looking I could not help but start to cry for her.

"Cecily, we are here for you. Where are the people that are doing this to you?" I asked.

All she could do was point behind us. There were figures approaching us. Sam whispered in my ear

"I will take care of them, get her out of here," and he was gone.

As I fumbled through my backpack for my majick book to look for a spell to try to get Cecily out of the prison, I felt breathing on the back of my neck. I looked over at Cecily and she had fear in her eyes.

"We've been waiting for you," someone whispered.

Three things happened at one time. One: I quickly turned around to see who it was. Two: I tripped on my backpack and fell flat on my face. Three: A black bag was placed over my head and I felt an excruciating pain on the back of my head as I passed out.

17 BETRAYAL

Netasha uncovered my head and let me see her face.

"Sophia, how nice of you to finally wake up," she said.

"You know, for a Flesh Craver, you really are easy prey."

Disoriented and dizzy, I looked up at her. She had me tied to a chair with those eyelash web thingies.

"Netasha, what do you want from me?" I asked. She let out a creepy kid giggle only a creepy kid could let out.

"What do I want from you? That is a great question. At first, I was happy you came for me. Being an original born Flesh Craver must be great. You are just born with it. Having to go through this orientation has been such a drag. My gift, speaking with the dead you know, has its benefits. I have been visited by many lost souls who told me you were coming for me. To "recruit" me, they said. They told me to accept. You were my ticket in. And for that, I thank you."

"I want out of F.L.E.S.H. I want in with the Slankium organization. They can help me better than you can. From what I have heard though, you can't just walk in there and ask to be accepted. They have to want you. I figured you were the best one to help me out here. Weak little Sophia with so much to lose. Slankium folk are awesome. I heard Solhava gave you a run for your money at one time. Hah! You're so weak. I don't ever want to go back to the earth realm. Stupid humans with stupid lives. I don't want to be a Flesh Craver. Oooh. Look at me. I crave flesh. Take me to the powerful ones. The ones that will teach me the skills to succeed. Now that I am here, I want to be transferred. Make it happen. Now."

While she was talking, I was looking around the cave. This was a dark damp room and in every corner, shadows danced in the light of the wall torches. Some gurgling sounds were coming from the cracks and crevices in the walls. I don't ever want to know what's back there. Where was Sam? Hannah? Jeremy? I hoped they were okay.

Just as my eyes were looking for a way out, Netasha jumped in.

"Oh would you just stop it. No one is going to save you. Your little friend Sam is unconscious in another room and Cecily is still in her cell. You know, her hair is fantastic! Who knew river fairies' hair had such meaning?" she exclaimed.

Oh no, she found out. How could she possibly know? Only river fairies know their hair had dozens of majickal capabilities and they do not share that information with just anyone. If made into a tonic, that tonic has the ability to bring back the dead.

Don't really know exactly what is DONE with the tonic, but Cecily had confided in me some of the river fairy secrets. But who would Netasha want to bring back from the dead?

"I'm really getting bored now. Here's the deal. Get me a real transfer from F.L.E.S.H. to Slankium and you are all free to go. Of course, you are not to say a word of this to anyone. If you don't comply, well, you're going to have to see some of your little buddies suffer a bit. I hear river fairies are deathly allergic to peaches?"

After she said this, a smile formed on her face. Not just a smile, but a twisted, demented smile. She was going to kill Cecily.

"Netasha, I don't even know if a genuine transfer can be made. You should know by now from the beginning of your orientation that we don't make deals with the Aerugian Corporation. They have proven irresponsible and untrustworthy. This goes way beyond my control. If we can't talk to anyone there, how do you expect me to make some sort of deal for you? What do you have to offer that other beings from other realms can't already give them? Why didn't you kidnap someone else? I don't have time for this nonsense!"

Okay. I was getting angry. Here was this little human teenager, threatening me. A Flesh Craver! Cecily, a river Fairy. Sam, a Scenter. We have to be better than this right?

"Hmmm… Interesting," she said.

"I didn't expect this from you. I really thought you cared about your friends. Maybe Cecily isn't all that important to you. But what about Jeremy?"

I winced. She knew she struck a nerve.

Now, it's not that Cecily was not important to me, I mean she's like my sister. They both hold different places in my heart and if she

expected me to choose, she had another thing
coming.

"Ouch," she said.

"So that's what it takes huh? Jeremy.
Jeremy. Let's see, where is Jeremy?"

She walked over to a small table with an
oil lamp on it and was talking to someone.

I couldn't see who she was talking to, but
I only assumed it was one of her lost souls.
While she was preoccupied, I had to think.
Where was my backpack? I had my majick book in
there and if I could just get to it, I could
try to find something that would help me out
here.

"Now, you stay here and keep an eye out on
our dear Sophia while I go fetch me some
peaches," Netasha said.

"Netasha, please. Don't do this. I can help
you. I can try. Please don't hurt Cecily."

"Oh, sweet Sophia. I'm not going to hurt
Cecily. Yet. I'm going to bring you a
surprise. Let's just say, a dear pal of mine
is helping me get what I need."

She walked through the protected shield of
the cell as if it weren't there. A small gust
of wind crept up beside me, and one of
Netasha's lost souls swooped in. It smelled of
dust and decay. It was transparent and solid.
It wore a black cape and wisped around me in
circles. The other lost soul had followed her
out of the cell, ready to complete its
mission.

"Shh. Your time will come soon. Soon the
Drünods will arrive and will collect what they
were promised. For now, comply with the girl."

Its voice sounded like nails on a
chalkboard. I closed my eyes. I didn't want to
look at this creature any longer.

I reached out to Sam. To Max. Help.
Anybody. Help. If you can hear me, I'm in an
underwater cave and Netasha is behind it all.
Sam, Max, can you hear me? Sam, are you all
right? Instantly, I could smell Sam. The scent
of fresh firewood filled the room. The lost
soul, mouth agape, managed to let out a big
sigh just before it exploded into non-
existence. Sam walked through the force field
with his hand stretched out. He was muttering
spell after spell under his breath. His eyes
lit up the room in a brilliant grey flash and
his growls became as loud as hurricane winds.

"Sam! Thank Hiliad you are here! Help me
out of this chair!"

Sam raced over to me and removed the lacey
bands that were beginning to slice through my
flesh.

"Sophia, we need to get these cells opened.
All of them. We need to release these
prisoners. I overheard Netasha and she is
something wicked. Come on, let's go."

We raced over to each cell, and with each
breath he took, Sam unlocked and freed all
prisoners, including Cecily. I hugged Cecily
as tight as I could as she fell into my arms
out of sheer exhaustion.

"Soph," she muttered. "I knew you would
find me. I just knew it."

And she passed out. Sam opened his pocket
mirror and one by one, he Reflectioned all
prisoners back to their safety. When Sam came
back after Reflectioning the Vandion, he had
a nice slice on his arm. When he came back
after Reflectioning the pleaser, he was
covered in blood.

"That son-of-a-bitch wanted me to feed off
of him. Ugh. I hate Pleasers so much."

"Sam, have you found Jeremy and Hannah?"

Sam was still mumbling all sorts of spells. He broke for a moment.

"Listen Sophia. I found them, but you need to prepare yourself. They aren't doing so well."

He continued to mumble his spells.

"What?" I yelled.

"Where are they? What's wrong with them?" Sam continued to lead me down another hall and continued to release prisoners from their cells.

I was so engrossed in thinking of what was happening to Jeremy I didn't realize just how many prisoners were down here. And just how many beings I didn't recognize. There were trapped lost souls, mermaids, and a Daeitimeny.

Wait. She had a Daeitimeny? And there was something else in that cell. I got a closer look and from what I could tell, it was a Flesh Craver. Could this be Dr. Trimon? How long have these beings been held captive here?

Sam released all of these beings and Reflectioned them all away. He was only gone for a second at a time, and I really began to see Sam how he wanted me to see him. He was a hero. The number of lives he just saved was enormous. There must have been hundreds of captives down here. With each Reflection, you could see a couple dozen Drünods waiting to catch him. Sam was too fast. Sam was too smart. And Sam needed to get me to Jeremy and Hannah now.

We reached the last of the cells and were down to only one. One? Why only one? As I pushed past Sam, he mumbled a spell and dropped the majick shield. I walked into complete darkness towards the back of the cell. I could smell flesh and blood all over the place. My hunger immediately started to take over. I glanced back at Sam and he was protecting the entrance to the cell. Where was Netasha? Why wasn't she intervening these escapes?

I remembered one of the spells we learned early on in our studies and lit up the room with a glowing ball of light. There, in the back of the cell, were Jeremy and Hannah. Jeremy was covered in blood and Hannah was on the floor. She wasn't moving.

I raced over to Jeremy and hugged him. He put his arms around me and sighed. This hug did not feel familiar. He felt stoic. He was smelling me. He did not speak. He was groping me. His hands were in my hair, holding my head and shoulders so close to his body I could feel every arch of his chest. He pushed me away and retreated. He flipped out on me. He went crazy.

He didn't want me touching him. He yelled for me to get out, to get back. He scrambled to the back of the cell, centering himself in the darkness. I could only see the glow of his eyes. I had to move my light a little closer to him to get a better view.

As I inched toward him, he looked up at me and growled. Mother of Hiliad, he growled. Not the Sam growl. A different growl. His hair was draped across his face in a mess of sweat and blood. It was sticking to his cheeks, creating a grotesque mask around his features. His mouth was open, and he was drooling. A lot. He had flesh glued to his chin and it was slipping down within the drool.

He looked up at me our eyes met. His

beautiful eyes. The eyes that captured my heart from day one. The same eyes that gave me a glimpse of happiness, something I had not felt in a very long time.

Those eyes. However, these eyes were no longer his. These eyes glowed a deep orange, a fire orange, almost red. A color so scary you had to look away before it sucked you into the depths of hell. This was the new Jeremy. It was at that moment that I knew. I knew, looking into his newborn eyes, he was no longer human.

Sam saw the look on my face and came racing in. He grabbed me just in time to swoop me out of the cell and put the shield back up before Jeremy lunged at me, biting the air, clawing at the shield and growling. His eyes continued to glow within the faint light that was in the room, and he was psychotic. He was like an animal. Hannah's body lay limp on the floor behind him. I crept into Sam's arms and cried.

"Sam, what's wrong with him? Is Hannah dead?"

Sam tried to comfort me.

"Sophia, Jeremy is going through a transition right now. Hannah is not dead, but close to it. He is guarding her body as his kill. He does not know what is happening to him, but there is no reversal. Netasha set this all up and I am so sorry. We need to get you out of here so that I can get him out."

"I'm not going anywhere without him Sam!"

I yelled. Sam continued reciting his spells to keep Netasha and her clan at bay, and all I wanted was to hold Jeremy in my arms and explain to him everything would be all right. It had to be all right, right? I mean, Sam said, we were meant to meet. We were meant to fall in love. He didn't stop it from happening.

"Sophia, I can't help him with you here. He wants to hurt you. I need to get you somewhere safe. I need to get you back to F.L.E.S.H. or back to Max."

I know what Sam was saying made sense, but I didn't feel right leaving him and Hannah. Jeremy continued to race and attack the barrier, trying every which way to get to me. With every launch, he cracked into the shield and fell back onto the damp floor of the cell. He didn't seem to feel pain. He howled in frustration, drooling and snarling in my direction.

Sam opened up his pocket mirror and he Reflected us to F.L.E.S.H. before I could put up any more of a fight. We were in a training studio and the room was empty. At this time, the building was deadville. You could see the occasional ogre cleaning up the hallways, but not much else. "Max!" yelled Sam.

"Max come here now."

Max appeared in his Heavenly glow and slammed onto the floor. He was clearly pissed. "Sophia, where did you go? Why did you run away from Sam? I couldn't even sense you!" Sam paced the room, running his hands through his hair and mumbling under his breath.

"Sophia thought she could fix this herself. She just wanted to find her friends. SHE wasn't thinking. SHE was getting herself into more trouble without thinking of the rest of us who are trying to HELP her."

Sam sat on a chair and stared at me. His eyes were fading in and out – grey, brown, grey, brown. I could feel his heartbeat in the room and could hear his breathing. He was not happy.

"Sophia, I hate to do this to you, but I'm going to have to secure you someplace safe until we get this under control," Max said. I looked up at him in horror.

"Max no! You're not taking me anywhere! I need to be here, helping you. I need to be here for Jeremy and Hannah. And Netasha only wants to talk to me. She will continue hurting people if I don't do what she says." I pleaded with him, but it seemed as if Max and Sam had their minds made up. They were ganging up on me, and I couldn't take them down.

"I'm truly sorry for this Sophia," said Max. As he said this, he placed his hand over my mouth and all went black.

18 TRUTHS

Truth can be a tricky thing. One minute, you think you know someone and the next minute, they betray you. How do I know this? Well, I have been undead for many years and for many years, I have trusted. I have trusted good people and trusted people I should have run from the moment I met them.

While I was in my paralysis state in some nether realm Max had generously bestowed upon me, I had time to think. I thought of the many people that have come into my life. The people that are gone and the people that are still here. How many of them do I confide in? How many can I call family?

There's Cecily, my bestest friend. She has been there for me through thick and thin. She has seen me at my worst, well, in relationships anyway. She has seen me at my best. She has never judged me and I loved her for that. Hannah, she has been a mentor, a guide; somewhat like a mother.

Since my parents passed away so many years ago, I was lacking that parental guidance. When my calling struck me as a Flesh Craver, they knew. They told me at a very young age. I had siblings, and they too have since passed. However, I have nieces and nephews that don't want to know me. They don't want to be a part of my Craver life.

I have never really understood why people choose the paths they do and shun family. I never hurt anyone. Well, except the beginning stages of my craver transition and then there was that brief moment in Pleasers Alley, but that's it! Um, hello! Why don't I have more family? What have I been afraid of all these years? The loss? The fear of the loss?

I have tried to look my family up. Sometimes, I Reflection into their homes and look at them. Do they look like me? Do they act like me? What are their lives like? I know what you're thinking. I am a stalker. But I'm really not. I still feel that sense of loss. Like I have missed out on so much because of my calling.

True, I had a distant relative in The Lost Petals that was called not too long ago. She knows OF me, just hasn't gotten the courage to confront me. Why? Why are we so AFRAID? I have to remember to get in touch with her when I get through this. Family is important.

Well, it's all starting to come into perspective now. The truth is I am at risk of losing the only family I really have. Because of me. I still don't understand Netasha's game plan, or why she chose me, but either way, it was BECAUSE of me that Cecily, Jeremy and Hannah were in danger. And Max and Sam were out there, somewhere, fighting for me.

This plane was special. It was soothing. I don't exactly know where I was, but I was alone. It was quiet. Peaceful. I sat down on silky pink grass and closed my eyes. It was time for some deep thinking. How would I save my friends? How would I save my boyfriend?

What did Sam mean when he said Jeremy was "transitioning" and that it wasn't reversible?

I had never seen anything like it. Jeremy had been acting like an animal. A rabid, drugged, crazed animal. And he was after me. He did not seem too interested in attacking Sam. He had already gotten to Hannah. Oh, Hannah. I hope you are all right. Please Hiliad. If you can hear me, please let them all be okay.

It all started with Netasha. The first day I got her and we went through Reflection World was the first day I saw the Drünods. They weren't interested in me that first time around. What were they doing? We got into Reflection World, I saw Jeremy, and then I saw a cemetery. The figures were above a body.

That's right! It was Netasha's body! Contorted and disfigured. The Drünod also spoke to me. What did it say Sophia? What did it say? Think! It's voice rang in my ears so loud I jumped. "Shh, you will wake the child," it had said. I remember very clearly now.

What did that mean? Why didn't I look into that a little more? When I had asked Netasha about those figures, she didn't seem concerned at all. Did she know about them already? Ugh! I was starting to get more and more frustrated. I couldn't do this alone. I needed Sam and Max. I needed to get into the F.L.E.S.H. caves and do some research. I clearly needed HELP!

"Maaaaaaaaxxxx," I yelled.

"Maaaaxxxx come back to me. I can help. I remember some stuff that can help."

Alright alright alright! I didn't really have a good case there calling him, but I didn't want to be here anymore. I still needed to go to the caves and try to get more information.

"Maaaxxxxxxxxx!" I yelled at the top of my lungs, but nothing happened.

I was growing impatient. What was going on? How was Jeremy? And Hannah? Where was Sam? Evan? I walked around, hoping to find something, anything. A house. A building. A shack. It was empty. The pink fields were never-ending. The trees swayed back and forth in the non-existent breeze. There were four suns overhead, but the temperature was cool. I could see stars and planets just above me. Slowly but surely, insects came out of hiding and fluttered by, creating small gusts of wind that tickled my face.

As I continued to walk with anger and anxiousness, I was getting tired. My back was itchy and it was only then that I realized I was carrying my backpack. My backpack! My majick book! Thank you sweet Hiliad! You saved me! What Sam and Max didn't know was that I had a small mirror in my majick book. You know, sometimes you needed to Reflection into another realm for a few spells.

I threw my backpack down creating a dent in the perfect pink grass. The grass seemed to sigh at me as if I had injured it. I pulled the majick book out of my backpack and opened it to the middle of the book. There was my mirror, beautiful and waiting for me. I did not have time to worry about how mad Sam and Max would be at me for leaving. All I could think of was to help them in any way I could. I quickly studied some spells and against my better judgment, I entered Reflection World alone.

As soon as I entered Reflection World, it

was as if an alarm had been set off. Sirens went off all around me and Drünods were racing in my direction. I focused on my mission and quickly headed toward my light and outran them. I did it! I didn't get caught!

When I exited Reflection World, I ended up at the entrance to the caves. Our cavearian Frank was sitting at his station, reading a book.

"Hi Frank, how's it going?" I asked.

I was trying to remain calm so that I wouldn't alarm him. He was a Flesh Craver, yes, but he was also a braken. A braken is a being that can sense anxiety. This was extremely helpful because if someone were coming in here to steal something, he can sense it right away.

"Sophia my dear. Good to see you. You have not been here for a while now. Did you finally manage to see the bright side and start dating that lanky gentleman? What is his name? Sam, is it? Oh that fella, he has it bad for you."

Frank giggled when he said this as he pushed his glasses above the edge of his nose. He was a jolly fella, old. Not sure how old, but old. And established. He knew his majick and knew it well. His salt and pepper hair curled around the frame of his face.

"Frank, I'm not dating Sam," I gasped.

I too giggled. Frank was nice, sweet. Grandfather-like.

"Well dear, don't let time slip past you. He's a good one, that Sam. Unless you have found another with a cleaner soul, he's a winner."

He looked up at me above his wire rimmed reading glasses and his eyes twinkled. I looked away to avoid eye contact.

"Okay Frank, um, well, I'm just gonna peruse the caves a little bit to learn some more of my history. Are the untranslated sections still closed off? Man oh man I have been dying to see the artwork in there!"

I tried to be slick. I tried to act normal.

"Yes my dear. They are still closed off. As long as you stay on the trail, you should be well on your way to enlightenment. Learn well."

Frank went back to his book. I quickly walked past him with my notebook in my hand. Suddenly, I felt a hand on my shoulder.

"Sophia, dear. I sense you are…troubled. Is everything going well?"

Frank asked with concern on his face. He towered over me and holy crap I was going to get caught.

"Um, no Frank. Everything is not going well. You see, here's the thing. I'm having a bit of an issue with Drünods. I was hoping I could find something in the cave art to help me understand their purpose."

Frank studied my face and frowned.

"What is it you need to know? Surely you don't think that you can translate the cave art, do you? We have many, many experts in and out of these caves, engineers and scientists work on these caves every day. If you think for one second I would allow you to enter the forbidden sections, you are sadly mistaken."

He was stern, and a little scary. His nostrils flared with the beginning signs of anger and frustration.

"Um, no Frank. That's so not my intention. I know I'm nowhere near the intellectual level of these experts. I was just hoping to go through the already translated sections to see if I can learn some more on the Drünods. I have to find a way to get them off of my back."

Frank studied my face once again, and his hand was still on my shoulder. He closed his eyes and took a deep breath. He walked over to his desk, made a phone call and Trina appeared. Trina was the other cavearian.

"Hello Frank. I will stand watch for you now," said Trina. Frank put his arm around my shoulders and walked with me through the entrance of the cave.

"You see Sophia, throughout many, many years we have been working on a way to develop a peaceful world. A world in which beings from all planes could co-exist with harmony. We have found many successful spells and guidelines within the walls of these caves. We have discovered ways of getting to hundreds of realms, some of which are quite scary, only to succeed in educating and recruiting."

"We are now a subject in most otherworld schools you know. However, there are still thousands upon thousands of untranslated texts, waiting for us to be ready to understand and accept their meanings before we are graced with the power and knowledge to translate them. Now, from the looks of things, you have not been keeping up to date on your studies. Knowledge is the key to our survival."

"Take this piece here. Do you know what this symbol means?" Frank asked.

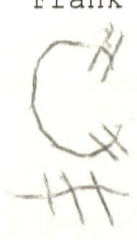

He covered the meaning of the symbol, which was in fine print underneath the display. I knew the symbol well. It was inscribed in everything I owned at F.L.E.S.H. It was the only symbol on the front page of my bible!

"Of course Frank! This is the Flesh Craver symbol. It's on everything we have. It's the only symbol on the cover of our Essentials and Fundamentals of Flesh Collection book."

I shouted. Hey, I was happy I knew something. He was testing me.

"Very good Sophia. Very good. Now, as we have learned from our history…"

Frank kept talking, and I zoned. I should have been paying attention to him, but my mind kept wandering back to Jeremy. How vicious he looked. How hungry he was to tear me to pieces. He wanted to hurt me. I have never felt so hurt or betrayed. I know it wasn't him. I know whatever transformation he was going through, he was in there, somewhere, trying to stop this beast from killing me (or tearing me to pieces).

"Sophia, pay attention. I'm not doing this for my good looks," snapped Frank. I refocused on his words and teachings. He continued.

"The following symbol is the oldest symbol we know of. This is the great Goddess Hiliad. Hiliad is the one who granted majicks to those who were worthy. You know, Sophia, this is where the Forever curse came from." I looked at the symbol.

So elegant. So beautiful. Goddess Hiliad.

The one we have to thank for all of this. Thanks a lot Hiliad. Thank you for allowing me to be undead. Thank you for ripping a perfectly good human life right out from under my feet so that I could "live" through this nightmare you call the craver "life". Yes. Sarcasm. I've said it before.

Being a Flesh Craver is bittersweet. There are some benefits, but mostly, I would love nothing else than to live on the earthly realm and exist for, oh, say eighty years and die with dignity.

"Snap out of it Sophia. Do you want me to help you or not?"

Frank scolded me for the last time. He looked down at me and pointed his finger in my face.

"Listen, you have Drünods coming after you. They are not a joke. One thing you must learn is there is someone out there controlling them. What are the reasons behind their motives? Why have they chosen you? What you think you know let it go. It is not that simple. You must learn your history to understand the now. Let us get to the truth. Let's get you out of this mess."

Frank continued his lecture.

"Goddess Hiliad is one of six of the higher power Goddesses in our realm. She alone grants us permissions for many majicks. Of course, our majicks come with a price. We must use them wisely. Hiliad is the Goddess we seek answers and guidance from. She is the Goddess of wisdom, purity and love."

"There are five remaining Goddesses that are not so wise and pure. They must remain a united power in order to keep the realms from merging and chaos from ensuing. The other five Goddesses are depicted here."

 Enthynie - Goddess of the Elements

 Julerion - Goddess of Pain and Suffering

 Oesphines - Goddess of Strength

 Ravoira - Goddess of Peace and Tranquility

 Silpanie - Goddess of Life and Death

As Frank pointed out the symbols of the six

Goddesses, I gazed upon them with wonder and fright. These were the beings we prayed to. These were our higher beings.

"Frank, why did we choose Hiliad to worship and not any of the others?" I asked.

Hey, it was a genuine question. Sure, one I should have known the answer to, but a valid question nonetheless.

"Sophia, it is not solely Hiliad we worship. Hiliad works with the other Goddesses and they come together in their decision making. They reserve the rights to choose who suffers, who lives, who dies and who is strong enough to handle power, pain, and love. Hiliad guides us in the right direction with her wisdom, but ultimately, the choices are ours to make. Is this not something you were taught very early on in your Flesh Craver beginning courses?" he asked.

Yeah, he got me. But it's been so long. And really, who worships and prays anymore? I mean, Hiliad hasn't really graced me with super majickal powers, no matter how much I asked her to help me out in desperate times. What. Did. All. Of. This. Have. To. Do. With. Jeremy?

"Frank, thank you for taking the time to help me learn a little more. I appreciate everything you are doing for me. But you see, here's the thing. I am in a hurry. My boyfriend is sick. My two friends are out there right now trying to save him from an underwater cell. We know who released the Drünods on me. I just need help figuring out how I can get the Aerugian Corporation to talk to me so that I can ask Slankium if they would accept someone into their organization."

As soon as those words left my mouth, Frank

backhanded me across my cheek

"Child. You will not have any dealings with Aerugian or Slankium. What is wrong with you?" he asked, huffing and spitting in sheer anger. Where he slapped me hurt. He was strong. He hit part of my nose and it bled.

"Frank, um, it's not for me. You see, the person who is doing this to me wants me to get them into Slankium or they will continue to hurt my friends. I have to do something."

I put my palm on my cheek and wiped the blood away from my nose. It had traveled down to my lips and I licked the rest away.

"Sophia, know this. Once you have dealings with Aerugian Corporation, you will immediately be disposed of by F.L.E.S.H. You will no longer be a part of our peaceful world and you will be destroyed – cast out like a traitor. There is no reason on all of the realms to deal with them. No reason."

He took a step back and put his head down. Taking off his glasses and rubbing his eyes, he sighed.

"Sophia, I love you like a granddaughter. Like my own flesh and blood. I once made a promise to myself to watch over you. To make sure you were not getting yourself into trouble, much like your mother did when she was your age. You must not do this."

"Frank. Tell me how to get rid of the Drünods. Once they stop coming after me, we can work on getting to the bottom of it all."

He shook his head. "You don't understand my dear. It is not the Drünods you need to be afraid of. It is the person behind the Drünods you must fear. The Drünods do not attack unless told to do so."

"Okay Frank. What do we need to do to the

being that is behind the Drünod attacks? We need to move quickly!"

He cocked his head to the side and grinned.

"Sophia, dear. Do you ever really know someone? Do you ever think to yourself 'man, am I gullible'? Because, you see, all of this time spent in these caves, we could have been out there, helping Sam and Max with Jeremy. Yet you continue to delay the battle."

Frank's face changed. His features became twisted and warped and he dropped to the floor of the cave. Trina ran over to help him.

"Sophia, what have you done to him? What have you done to him?" She continued to throw evil glares my way and focused on Frank.

"I...Trina...I don't understand." I mumbled.

She had no interest in speaking to me.

"Frank, Frank wake up. Frank."

I backed away through Trina's screams. She removed his glasses and opened his eyes. She inspected his mouth. From her pocket, she removed a small white shiny stone. She placed it in his mouth and whispered an incantation. Instantly, a shadow crept out from beneath Frank's body and flew out of the caves.

"Sophia, you need to leave. Now. You never should have come here. You have brought nothing good to F.L.E.S.H. Leave!"

She yelled at me and lifted her hand with her palm facing me. A violet light came rushing out of her palm and hit me directly in the chest, knocking me into the wall.

"Trina, I'm so sorry. Is Frank all right?"

I said.

She twisted her head my way and didn't have to utter a word. I got it. I backed out of the cave, crying.

Trina was a Flesh Craver. But she was also a siren. Sirens are not all that nice, but if you make them angry enough, they can really hurt you.

I was alone again.

I was afraid again.

Now, I didn't even want to call to Max or Sam because I escaped Max's world. I heard Frank's words in my head, over and over again. 'It is the person behind the Drünods you need to fear,' he had said.

Netasha.

I decided to step up my game and stop acting like a child. I needed to save the day. With my majick book in hand, I Reflectioned to the Galariyan Oceans and entered the underwater caves. I felt alive and my mission was clear.

I needed to kill Netasha.

19 REVELATIONS

With my newfound courage, I scaled the halls of the caves like a champ. Every little noise, I muttered a spell here and a spell there to try to kill it. Sure, my spells were mediocre, but they did the trick. Like, you know, killing that drop of water. And, you know, eviscerating that little water fly.

When I reached the end of the caves, the cell that had held Jeremy and Hannah was empty. In fact, this entire place was empty. Not one blessed being. Not one ounce of danger. I was done. My courage ended here.

Putting my tail between my legs, I called out to Max. He appeared right away with his arms across his chest. He didn't say anything to me. I dropped to the ground and sobbed.

"Max, I don't know what to do. I feel like everything is crashing down around me and I don't know how to fix it." He looked down at me and lifted me up.

"Shhh, Sophia. I will make everything better."

He wrapped us up in his silky Angelic wings

and transported us out of the caves. When Max unwrapped his wings, I took a good look at our surroundings. We were back at the caves of F.L.E.S.H. What? Why were we here? He still had me in his arms and carried me through the dim halls of the cave.

I noticed all of the lanterns went dark as we went past them.

"Max, where are we going?" I managed to mutter through tears. He didn't speak.

"Max. Where are we going?" I asked again, with a little more force this time.

Max continued to walk his Angelic walk, but I noticed he was different. He didn't ooze the love and care. He didn't look at me with concern and adoration.

"Max?" I asked. I touched his wings. They felt warm. Almost too warm.

Usually Serminian Angels' wings are light, feathery and at just the right temperature.

"Max, put me down." Again, he ignored me.

"Max, put me down right now!"

I had no choice but to start flailing around like a crazy craver.

Max held on to me with one arm. He had the strength of a million cravers. As he walked me through the forbidden paths of the caves, through my flailing I saw dim lights up ahead. Suddenly, I smelled firewood. Sam!

I had never been so happy to smell Sam. We got closer and closer to the firewood smell, and I spoke to Sam in my mind.

"Sam, please tell me you can hear me. Max has gone mad." Sam shushed me.

"Sophia, it's not Max. Don't freak out."

Max, or the not Max, tossed me to the ground in front of a cell. Great, another cell. Sam yelled into my mind "run!" So, I did.

Not Max just stood there, staring at me running. He didn't try to come after me. As I looked back at him, I ran into someone. Netasha. She was laughing.

"Netasha, stop. I will help you against everything I stand for. I will talk to Slankium if you want me to. Just give me the opportunity."

Netasha opened her eyes wide, huge, as if they would just pop out. She pointed at me, and laughed some more.

"Max, be a dear and get Sophia into that cell. Oh, you can put her in with her precious Jeremy. That's right. Jeremy is here. Sam, brilliant Sam, you are going to Slankium to get them to get me in. You see, I have no intention of keeping any of you alive. Not even the Angel. He's powerless now. He is possessed by my lost soul. I came to realize that Sophia isn't the one with so much to lose, it's you. If you are not back here in one hour, they all die."

Not Max threw me into a cell and sure enough, Jeremy was in there. This time though, he was tied to the very back wall in some heavy chains.

"Go ahead Sophia, give him some sugar," she said and laughed and laughed.

Sam spoke to me. "Sophia, I am going to do

this. I have no choice. I will try to be quick. Be careful in there. Max can't break free of his possession, not without Angelic intervention. Hannah is in the cell with me. I have tried to heal her. She doesn't look well."

"Sam" I said. "Please, be careful. Please come back."

Netasha let Sam out of his cell and he Reflectioned out of the caves. Netasha walked into his cell and kicked Hannah.

"Wake up. Wake up! I know you can hear me. Get up. You. You know how to translate these cave drawings. Let's go. You have work to do. One hour. I need to bring something meaningful to Slankium if I want in."

Hannah stood up. She had blood on the side of her face, and the sight of it made me hungry. Hannah steadied herself on her feet, looked over at me, and winked. Netasha led her to one of her lost souls who took Hannah away into the depths of another branch of the cave.

Jeremy was stirring behind me. He began his growls as he smelled my fear. I carefully walked over to him and Netasha's voice scared me from behind the cell shield.

"He's cute. He will be even cuter when he tears you apart. Why don't you just end it now for him Sophia? Why don't you end his pain? You see, he's suffering. The transition he is going through is quite the special one. It's not complete yet. He can still be killed."

I listened to her and watched him. He was

fighting to break free of the chains. He was snarling, growling, hissing and spitting. His once beautiful hair was thick with blood and dirt. He had blood all over his body, but for the life of me, I did not see one wound.

I spoke through gritted teeth.

"What have you done to him?" She bent over in laughter.

"Finally! Finally you ask! Sophia, meet Jeremy, your new boyfriend. Human no more. Flesh Cravers in all realms beware! You donoc, stupid girl. All of these years you have had to learn everything and anything about the craver life and beings from other realms, and you chose to spend your time reminiscing about the good old human days. Guess what? A lot has changed in the Craver world."

Netasha's eyes lit up. She seemed too eager to continue this conversation. I definitely had a bed feeling about this. She continued.

"Starting today. Jeremy is now transitioning into the first known Flesh Craver that is a Flesh Craver hunter. The cave drawings said it all. The spell was there. But, there's a catch. Not one single being has ever survived the spell. I don't know if Jeremy will, but he sure has lasted longer than everyone else. If he does survive, which I really hope he does, he will be the first of his kind, his breed. They are called Perditors. You know them right? I mean, I'm sure you at least paid attention to what could kill you. The Forever curse potion, some oddball beings here and there, and a Perditor."

My undead heart sank. Not Jeremy. He can't be a Perditor! They are only a legend. No one has ever been successful in creating them. Perditors I do know of. We were taught, way back when in Flesh Craver 101, Perditors, if ever created, would equal the destruction and extinction of all Flesh Cravers. This can't be true!

Immediately I called out to Sam.

"Sam, can you hear me. Please, Netasha turned Jeremy into a Perditor. He needs your help."

Sam replied in an instant.

"No one can save him Sophia. I'm sorry. I will be there soon."

Netasha grinned. "So beauty queen, what are you going to do? Are you going to try to find the cure for him? Because I'm sure it is within the walls of this cave. Hannah! What's taking so long? Get me some translations!"

Netasha continued.

"Tick tock, Sophia. Tick tock. Sam has 20 minutes to get here with a Slankium representative. Hopefully Solhava. Man, that beast is a legend. To meet him would be out of this realm. TICK TOCK HANNAH!"

Hannah came back with the lost soul, bunches of papers in her bloody hands. The lost soul made her jot down the translations in her own blood.

"Here," said Hannah.

"Here are your precious translations. Obviously I can't get them all, but these should suffice to get you into Slankium."

Netasha snatched the pages from Hannah's bloody hands and looked them over. There were symbols and words all over the pages in bloody smears.

"Nice. Nice. Oooh. I like this one. This spell teaches us how to possess Wentinian Angels. Sweet! Serminian Angels, piece of cake. Wentinian Angels, now, they are nasty. What are they now? The Angels of the dark lord? This is some good stuff Hannah. Get back in your cell. You're no good to me now."

The lost soul breezed it's way around Hannah and tossed her into the cell. She fell over a small table that was in there and twisted her leg. I heard her cry out in pain.

"Hannah!" I yelled. Netasha cut me off. "Oh Oh. Guess who got one of the chains off. Take a peek behind you."

I turned around and Jeremy had broken his wrist and had one hand free of the chains. He was working on the other one, trying to tear it off the wall. The wall was crumbling, little rocky chunks and dust falling all over the place He was a fighter.

I could see him a little clearer now. His face was blackened with dirt and dried up blood. He was growing fangs and they were starting to peek out from under his upper lip. His once beautiful honey colored eyes were now the color of fresh embers. He looked over my way.

His look was sad. For a moment, I saw Jeremy

in there. His eyes went from fiery embers to the color of beautiful smooth honey. His arms fell to his sides and he moved the hair that covered his face. He took a deep breath. "Sophia?" he asked. I ran over to him. I hugged him, and he hugged me back.

"Sophia, what is happening to me? I can't control it. It hurts. My visions are distorted now." He was scared.

"Jeremy, let me explain this to you quickly. Netasha has you transitioning into a Perditor. Killer of Flesh Cravers. You are transitioning into a Flesh Craver first, then you will complete your transition into the Perditor."

He held his broken wrist up to his heart and winced in pain. I noticed a small symbol on the inside of his wrist. This symbol was the Perditor symbol. That's it! I have seen that symbol before too. Where have I seen this?

"What? I don't understand. Why?"

He was confused and lost.

"She wanted to use me to get into Slankium and in order to get me to do what she wanted, she chose to hurt the ones I cared about the most. You were the only human, so you were the easiest target."

"But isn't she human too?" he asked.

"Yes," I said. But really, I was reconsidering that.

What human would do something like this? What type of human would hurt another human being in such a way to get what they wanted? If humans did behave this way, why would I want to go back to the earth realm?

I heard a click behind me and there stood Max. Non-Max. He stood like a robot and held something in his hands. As he got closer, I saw he was holding Sam's sword. The sword he had in his library. The same sword with which he had cut the Drünods' arm.

Jeremy held me tight. However, once he saw the sword, the symbol on the sword and the symbol on his wrist lit up. They were the same symbol! This was a Perditor sword. Jeremy instantly turned into a ravenous monster again and used his one hand to grab onto me.

His fangs seemed to have grown as he opened his mouth wide and took a bite out of my arm. Netasha giggled as she watched from outside the cell. Her minion lost soul was circling her, glowing white eyes and black cloak fluttering with each swirl.

I twisted Jeremy's arm just enough for him to let go of me and I hurled myself to the opposite side of the cell. My wound was not healing. I needed to collect, to feed. Not Max walked slowly toward Jeremy, swinging the sword back and forth as it dangled from his robotic arm. His face was stoic. His wings were fraying.

Jeremy battled with the chains. Battled to get to me. Battled to get to Max. From a distance, I heard Hannah's cries

"Sophia, get out of there."

At once, there was a tear in the shield to my cell, and my ears were covered in a slimy goo. Netasha's eyes grew wide and her mouth hung open as she struggled to understand what was happening. Her lost soul poofed into non-existence as Hannah wailed in their direction. Her wails were so loud they broke the shields completely from both of our cells, and Netasha's body lay limp on the ground of the cave.

I raced over to Hannah as Max continued his path toward Jeremy. Jeremy broke free from his last chain on his hands, but his legs were still chained. He flung himself at Max and I felt a swift cool breeze beside me. Sam Reflectioned back over to us. He stood there with Solhava, who had come to collect Netasha.

Max and Jeremy battled, and Jeremy broke free of his chains. Sam and Hannah chanted some spells and the shield was back up. Jeremy lunged toward me but Max stopped him. Solhava bent down to examine Netasha and noticed a small puddle just beneath her neck. He was holding a vial and collected the puddle.

It hit me like a ton of bricks. This was not Netasha. This was a Clider. Solhava collected his cave art translations and vanished with the vial.

Hannah, Sam and I watched as possessed Max and Jeremy battled. Jeremy tore Max's wings off, ligament by ligament. All that was left of them were bloody stumps and wing cartilage. Random feathers were sticking out of the cartilage like tiny broken wires. His wing feathers were all over the cell, and as they battled, the feathers were thrust upward in a swirl of bloody softness. You could hear the Grintan feathers' cries, for all of the fallen Angels they represented.

Max lifted the sword in a swift motion and sliced cleanly through Jeremy's wrist. His limp hand fell to the ground with a thump. I watched in horror as Max continued to slice through Jeremy's limbs, one at a time, incapacitating him from attacking him. Jeremy was able to get one last bite into Max's abdomen before falling to the ground, chewing hungrily at the newfound flesh. Max hovered over him for a moment, cocked his head, smiled and in a quick swoosh, he cut Jeremy's head off.

I screamed. Sam and Hannah held me down. Jeremy. This was Jeremy's vision, or part of it. He saw this happening and he couldn't stop it. He didn't understand how it would all come to be. The shield came down from the cell, and all that was left was Max.

He fell to the ground in a bloody heap, sword still in his hand. I raced over to Jeremy and held his head in my hands. Sobbing, I hunched over his destroyed body and my thoughts were going wild. What just happened? Why? Could I have stopped this if I had tried harder?

I prayed silently to our Goddess Hiliad to send me answers. Something, anything, to make this right. He can't be dead. I looked over at Hannah and Sam who were crouched down helping Max.

They helped him up after he regained consciousness and he was Max again. He had no idea what had happened. He glanced my way, looked at the sword in his hands and dropped it. He fell to his knees.

"Sophia. I…I…did I do this?" he asked.

He had so much sorrow in his voice. I nodded. What else could I do? I did not have the energy to explain this all to him. Hell, I didn't truly understand what happened either.

A blinding light lit up the room and another Angel appeared.

"I am Ambrosia, and I am here to collect my brother. He is in grave pain."

Ambrosia was beautiful. In fact, she looked like Sam's perfect little Angel wife from my visions in Reflection World.

"Thank you Ambrosia!" I whispered. "Please take care of him."

Ambrosia walked over to me and placed a hand on my chin.

"My child, Max's behaviors were not his own. He was a victim of a possession. Our brothers and sisters will heal him well. We will hold a trial for him regarding the deaths of the three gentlemen earlier. I am afraid that is all I can tell you."

She scooped Max up in her embrace as he stood limp in her arms.

"Ambrosia, thank you for coming. This was not me. This was not me." He pleaded.

He had an Angelic tear streaming down his face which left a slightly red trail as it burned its way down.

"Silence brother. We will aide you in your recovery until your trial begins. We will stand by your side."

She wrapped her Angel wings around both of them, cocooning them in her embrace, and they faded away in her light.

I looked down at the mess that was Jeremy. My undead heart was broken. I sat there, caressing his hair. Sam and Hannah were talking amongst themselves and Sam leaned down to reclaim his sword. He held it in his hands as if it were poison. Hannah walked over to me and crouched down.

"Sophia, listen to me. You must get up. We must leave right away. Sam will stay here to clean up this mess. You absolutely cannot be here. They are coming."

She met my eyes, and I began to cry all over again.

"Hannah, I can't just leave him. He is my love. We were supposed to meet. We were supposed to fall in love. Why did this all happen?"

She held me in her arms and I wept.

"Shh. Everything will turn out just fine Sophia. Please trust me. But we really must go."

I felt a small pinch on my arm and briefly

caught a glimpse of Hannah retreating with a syringe.

"Just go to sleep Sophia, and when you wake up, things will be much better."

The world went dark, and Hannah faded away.

20 HOPE

When I woke up, I was in my own bed, snuggled up in my comfortable sheets. Ah, this felt good. There was a knock on my bedroom door, and Cecily walked in with a warm cup of gooey bloody goodness for me. I devoured it within seconds.

"So sleepy head, how do you feel today?" she asked. Surprisingly enough, I felt wonderful. One of our many moons was shining a bluish light into my bedroom and I had never felt better.

"Cecily, I like your hair," I said. It was cute. You know, everything about Cecily is cute, but today, she looked simply adorable.

"You think? I don't know, I was thinking maybe it's too short." We chuckled.

Her pointy Fairy ears jutted out like perfect little pointy satellites, but she looked adorable just the same.

"I have a surprise for you," she said. She walked out of the room and came back in, skipping and hopping, with a box in her hands.

"Open, open, open!" she exclaimed Sheesh she was so excited. I guess I should open this before she exploded with Fairy giddiness!

I opened the box and inside was an envelope. I peeled back the wax seal and peeked inside. A small note card was neatly tucked away in the perfectly folded envelope. I quickly removed the card and began reading:

Sophia,

I wanted to write this letter to you to let you know I am okay. Sam's sword did not actually kill me. As it turns out, the only person who can wield that sword and utilize it's true powers, what it is truly meant for, is its rightful owner.

Sam was the only one who would have been able to wield the sword to seal my fate in death. Only the rightful owner knows this. Well, and me, and you, and Hannah, hah, and I assume Cecily. I am alive. Alive in that Flesh Craver/Perditor way anyway.

Hannah has begun teaching me some basic techniques to control my hunger for Flesh Cravers. So far, I am doing terrible, which is why I can't be with you right now. How I wish I could hold you in my arms, smell your hair, and comfort you. I miss you every second that goes by.

I will keep in touch with you, but I don't know how long I will be gone. I have asked Hannah to please keep an eye on you. You are quite the sneaky little craver. Keep yourself safe. I love you more than words can say.

Missing you like crazy,

Jeremy

Cecily was watching me the entire time I read the note. He was alive. He was really alive. Wait. How long was I asleep?
"Cecily, how long was I asleep?" I asked.
She looked away and was shaking her leg that was dangling off the bed. "Um, well, you were kind of asleep for about six months."
I leaped out of bed.
"Six months? I was asleep for six months? How? What? Why?"
I didn't even know where to begin.
"Well, you see, Hannah injected you with a serum for Flesh Cravers. It was meant to keep you whole, you know, keep you from rotting from not collecting and all, and keep you calm. She asked me to stay with you and told me when you would come to. I wanted to be here for you, to help you cope with what happened six months ago. So, go on, let me have it."
I wanted to be angry. I wanted to push Cecily out of the way and march over to Hannah's and demand she tell me where she was

keeping Jeremy.

"But, um, Sophia. There's one more thing. I haven't been the one to completely take care of you. I mean, I have been coming a day here, a day there, as much as my parents would allow me to anyway. There's one other person who has been with you this entire time."

Sam walked into my bedroom.

"Hey princess craver. We've missed you. Glad to see you are up and about."

Sam, a complete transformation from the Sam I knew all too well. Or not at all. Whatever.

"Sam, you've been taking care of me?" I asked.

"Uh huh," he mumbled. He looked away and sat on the edge of my bed.

"If you want me to go, I can go." I stopped him.

"No. Please don't go. I want you both to stay here, right now. Let me go freshen up and we can catch up on some things I'm still a little fuzzy with.

After I freshened up and we chatted for a while, Sam and Cecily left me to myself. I Reflectioned over to Hannah's, but did not demand she tell me where Jeremy was. She was right. He was right. I needed to give him his space. If he was going to learn to control his newfound powers, his new mission, he would have to do it without me. I walked over to F.L.E.S.H. and Evan greeted me at my cubicle. There were tons of flowers and little gifts at my desk. Welcome back and we missed you were written all over the sides of my cubicle.

I cleaned up most of my desk after Reflectioning all of the flowers back and forth to my apartment. When I returned, there was one more bouquet of flowers that had not been there before. A little box was sitting next to it with a note. I looked closer at the flowers and noticed they were bluish. As I inched closer, I felt the coolness of the flowers. They were the flowers from the Northern Ice Plains in the Freeze Dimension. What? How?

I opened up the box and in it was a stone. The stone had a symbol on it I had never seen before. I opened the letter.

Dear Sophia,

I hope you enjoy the flowers. I have been telling you over the years how much I love you and how much I so very want to be your one and only. I noticed you went through all of the letters I wrote you but never gave you. I made a promise to myself that day in the caves. When I saw you holding Jeremy in your arms, you were so sad. I did not know what to do that could take that pain away. The last six months have been difficult without you here. I have been studying and learning new things every day. I managed to save these flowers for you from the Northern Ice Plains. They will survive as long as you want them to.

In the box is a gift I have wanted to give you for so many years. I thought I would give this gift to you when you finally wised up and we were a couple. However, that day in the caves, the day you lost Jeremy, I had a second thought. Even though we are Flesh Cravers and will live essentially forever, forever just is not enough time. I want you to have this today. The stone is a Plinthe. This Plinthe is special. With the right spell, which I also enclosed underneath the stone, this stone will take you and one other person to another realm, a realm restricted to only Flesh Cravers.

The realm is also special in that there are many worlds within the realm. You and that other person will never have to share your space with anyone you don't care to share it with. Just think of the world you can create there for yourself. Peace, tranquility. Living a normal Craver life.

I had hoped we could live this life forever together, but I realize now that will never happen. I know your mission is to continue to wait for Jeremy, and I respect that. I suppose. I *still want you to have this stone, for if at any moment you choose to use it, I would hope you can use it for someone who means the realms to you.*

I won't make this weird. I promise. I figured I would write you this note instead of hand this to you in person so that I wouldn't, as you so eloquently phrase things, 'freak you out'. It's okay. I've made peace with your decisions.

My love for you burns brighter each day.

Always yours,

Sam

Sam.

There for me this entire time, Sam.

Has loved me all of these years, Sam.

I tucked the box with the stone and the spell in my purse, and placed the flowers on my desk. These flowers were staying here. Chloe waltzed into my cubicle holding a furry creature, and the familiar "mow" made me smile.

"Munchkin! Oh Munchkin, I have missed you so much!" I said.

Munchkin climbed elegantly onto my shoulders and perched on the back of my neck. All four sets of claws were glued into the first five layers of my flesh. I didn't care. Munchkin was the only thing I had left of my time with Jeremy.

Chloe smiled and did not say a word. She left just as quickly as she had entered, and I was quite okay with that. Everyone seemed to be walking on eggshells around me, but really, I felt wonderful. Even though I remembered every single detail of that traumatic day, I knew everyone was okay.

I opened my desk drawer and someone had placed my diary in it. There was a note. What is it with all of these notes! Why don't people just talk to me? The note simply said:

Please continue writing in your diary. This is the only way to write your history down for generations to read. We will get together soon to catch up. So many questions I would love to ask you. Your cousin, Helene.

Helene. That's a pretty name. She was right. I needed to get to writing. There was so much to write, I almost didn't know where to begin. I started writing.

Dear Diary,

The past year has been a doozy. I don't know, I kind of expected my life to be dull, boring. So much has happened. I will start with today. Today, I learned Jeremy was alive/undead, um, still with us. He is in a secret realm where Hannah and some of the Elders of F.L.E.S.H. are working with him to control his hunger for Flesh Cravers. They are taking extremely good care of him.

I miss him. I miss his eyes and his stubborn strands of hair. While I was visiting with Hannah, Max popped in to say hello. He had been fully healed and even got his wings back. His Angel brothers and sisters stood by his side during his trial, and in the end, the Creator felt Max had no other choice but to kill those three Scenters because they were secretly aiding Netasha, I mean, the Clider.

Max and Hannah explained it all to me. Netasha was dead before I even met her. The Clider had already infected the teenage girl I recruited. This Clider, who went by the name of Hrii, was the being who called the Drünods to attack me. Hrii wanted access to the caves to get the translations for the original spells to find a way to gain immortality for Cliders without having to constantly inhabit and steal the souls of other beings.

When Hannah killed its host, he did not have another able body to jump into and oozed out of the supposed Netasha shell. With the host dead, the Drünods were no longer directed to find and return me. There endeth my crazed hunger.

Solhava reached out to Sam a few days later and let him know he would turn Hrii into the counsel and have him stand trial, the judges being the six Goddesses. The Goddesses ended Hrii's life within five minutes of the trial starting. Solhava was awarded with some otherworldly powers for honesty and granted permission to leave Slankium to join F.L.E.S.H. with no further incident. He was now Sam's apprentice. Not sure how I feel about that. Solhava is a creepy fella. As long as he doesn't turn on me again, I suppose I am okay with it.

Sam was promoted to Senior Recruiter and Consultant for the Recruiting Division of F.L.E.S.H. He was granted access to some of the restricted sections of F.L.E.S.H. and was even given a series of tests to further his career. He is one happy craver, and I am so very proud of him.

Hannah allowed me to look into her mirror ball and I got a glimpse of Jeremy. He was meditating. There were two Flesh Cravers that volunteered to be bait to help him with his studies. They circled him as he sat on the stone patio of his home on this realm.

His eyes were closed, his breathing steadied. I watched him control his hunger for about five minutes before he tore the Flesh Cravers to pieces, killing them instantly. All that was left of them were their tattered, bloody, glomulis filled clothing.

Until tomorrow dear diary,

Sophia

    I tucked my diary in my purse along with my stone. I wrote a few letters and sent them along with the mail ogre. I uncovered my mirror and recited my spell. All was clear now. All was good. I knew what I had to do. I Reflectioned to Cecily's, placed a note on her dresser and plopped Munchkin on her bed.

    I gave Munchkin a kiss on her head and she purred for me. She looked up at me with those blue, blue eyes and I whispered to her I would come back for her.

24 DECISIONS

Sam walked into his cubicle with a skip and a jump. Sophia had to have seen her flowers by now, he thought eagerly. Why was she taking so long to come find me? He wondered. No worry. She will be here in no time.

As he rummaged through his case files, the mail ogre flung an envelope directly at his face. With quick reflexes, Sam caught the piece of mail with ease.

"Mail," yelled the ogre.

Seriously, we need to find some better employees here, Sam thought to himself.

The envelope had Sam's name on the outside. He fumbled the envelope open and read the contents of the letter:

Sam,

I want to thank you for everything you have done for me. You have showed me strength, courage and forgiveness. You have taught me to look on the inside, not solely on the outside. You have offered your life for me, and for that, I

235

can never truly repay you. When we merged, you let me into that part of you I had never seen before. This wonderful, amazingly talented and loving part of you. I will keep that memory stored away forever.

Please know I am doing this because I love him. From day one, I knew I loved him. You know this. You know this because you know how it feels to fall in love with someone at first glance. This is how I feel for him.

Remember: We can still find each other. We can still talk to each other. But, I need to be there for him. I need to help him overcome this new life he has ahead of him. I have my book of majick and I'm sure Hannah will get over her objections soon enough. She doesn't know I have located her spell on how to get to him, so I'm sure she will be a bit upset. I am going to stay with him, no matter how long it takes.

Please don't hate me. You hold a very special place in my heart. I will visit you from time to time. Take care of yourself.

Love,

Sophia

Sam held onto the letter with amazement. He thought for sure Sophia would come running to him. Her knight in shining armor. Her forever craver/Scenter. He thought for sure she would use the stone for the two of them. He closed his eyes and placed the letter back into its envelope. He tucked it into his pocket and looked over at his mirror. He called out to Sophia.

"Sophia, please don't go. I am begging you." She did not answer. Not right away.

"Sam, I am following my heart. Just as you were following yours all these years. I will be back, I promise."

Sam let her go. He knew she needed her space. She needed her time. She was in danger, for sure. Sophia did not know something about Jeremy. Something Hannah and Sam had decided to keep from her. Sam called Hannah and explained Sophia's letter. Hannah had received a letter as well. Hannah was prepared for stunt like this.

When Sam asked Hannah if she was going to intervene, she was silent. What Sophia did not know was that while Jeremy survived the curse to become a Flesh Craver/Perditor, part of the curse was poorly translated and activated. Jeremy was a Perditor, destroyer of Flesh Cravers, true.

He was also a new deity. Jeremy was not aware of this, but Sophia was not traveling to another normal realm to be with him. She was traveling to his realm, where he was now the ruler of his own kingdom. His powers would grow to great lengths.

Jeremy was still clinging to his humanity. F.L.E.S.H. elders were reaching out to Hiliad for suggestions on how to guide him. Hiliad consulted with the five other sisters and they determined Jeremy was a newly created entity, created by a spell gone awry. The elders had not prepared, even having access to some of the most amazingly talented majickal beings, to prevent this from happening. Therefore, the elders had to deal with the consequences and figure it out. Hiliad and the sisters refused to help.

EPILOGUE

Sophia walked onto the stone patio. All was silent. All was still. Every step she took, she heard a slight echo in the distance. The small stone house was set up high on the hill. There were beautiful circular stone columns framing the entrance to the home.

Huge flower pots were neatly and carefully placed to create a beautiful oasis of landscaping. The moons were shining bright. Crescent moon on the right, full moon above the house, and crescent moon on the left.

As Sophia opened the front door, she was greeted by three familiar faces. Flesh craver elders opened their eyes with amazement. They gasped at the sight of her. She smiled and continued walking to the back of the house. They followed quietly behind her, shuffling their old bare feet on the porcelain floors.

Sophia stepped out onto the back patio and spotted Jeremy right away. He was beautiful. He was wearing only a pair of jeans. His arms and chest were muscular and looked as solid as stone. Jeremy lifted his head and sniffed. He quickly turned his head toward Sophia. His honey eyes lit up and he raced over to her.

Jeremy picked Sophia up and kissed her deeply. He laughed and kissed her some more. No words needed to be spoken. They were together again. That is all that mattered. He carried her over and lay her gently under a tree. Its orange and blue leaves floated like petals under soft winds, collecting at the base of its crimson trunk resembling a painters' palette.

They lay there together, holding onto each other with all the love in the realms. Sophia turned to her side and looked into his eyes. His hair was doing that cute little thing again, and she was all too eager to remove the invasion from his beautiful face and tuck it behind his ear.

"I thought you were dead," said Sophia.

"I thought I lost you forever." She was still gazing into his honey eyes.

"I am here for you, always. Why did you come for me when I told you not to? You know I can't control the hunger forever, right?" said Jeremy.

"I know, but I can help you. I can be your strength. You don't want to hurt me, right? So you won't."

Jeremy leaned in and kissed her.

"Of course I don't want to hurt you. I don't know how to control it all just yet and I am afraid."

He traced his finger from her temple down to her chin. She felt a chill and giggled.

"Jeremy, trust me, everything is going to be just fine. We are here together, and nothing can stop us from making this work."

As Sophia continued to gaze into Jeremy's eyes, she was able to see his transformation. It happened quickly, almost too quickly for her. His eyes began to glow that amber, orangey red color. His breathing elevated. His fangs began to grow. He let out a loud growl and the elders raced down to protect Sophia.

"Why did you come here?" asked one of the elders.

"You should not be here. You are in grave danger."

As quick as a lightning bolt, Jeremy launched over and tore this elder to shreds. The other elders thought they were prepared. They recited many spells, however, none of them seemed to work. Jeremy mauled them just the same.

He leaned over their bodies and ate. Ate as if he had not eaten in years.
He turned to Sophia and the beast within him had taken over. He inched his way slowly in her direction. She had two options. Reflection out of here and get back to safety, or try to stop him. As he crept upon her, he was almost slipping on his own drool.

His face and mouth were caked with blood and bits of flesh. His fangs were dripping with saliva and blood. He was on all fours, eyes glowing, orange as can be. Brilliant red orange.

Sophia knew she was in trouble.

"Jeremy, relax. Jeremy, it's me, Sophia. Please don't do this. I love you. You have to reach way back inside of you. Find yourself."

She begged. She pleaded. Jeremy continued the slow slippery crawl in her direction. His growls grew louder as the distance between them grew shorter. Sophia felt a moment of regret. Had she made the right decision? It was too late to back out now. Sophia stood her ground as Jeremy pounced on her.

Her last vision before she closed her eyes were of Jeremy's eyes and the large fangs protruding from his mouth, fangs destined to destroy her.

ABOUT THE AUTHOR

Serendipity Bloom has always been intrigued by anything related to horror and zombies. As a little girl, she documented her dreams which eventually became the inspiration for her writing. She received her degree in Secondary Education in English and is currently pursuing a degree in Business Management. She enjoys painting, watching horror movies, and writing on her spare time. She currently lives in a small town in eastern Pennsylvania with her partner and probably one too many furry children.

You can find updates on Serendipity Bloom by visiting and liking her Facebook page at https://www.facebook.com/serendipity.bloom